LIVES OF CRIMES

John Scheck

Lives of Crimes

Published by **LEFTBANKER PRESS**

Copyright © 2025

Paperback ISBN: 979-8-9885351-8-8

VISITING DAY

I've tried to tally up exactly how much time I've spent inside of prisons. Not counting the few hours I spent in lock-up for a dismissed drunk driving offense when I was seventeen, I've been in two jails. All of my hard time comes on the days when I enter the gates to visit my incarcerated older brother.

If you've never visited someone in a federal prison, it's not something I'd recommend, although spending time in the visitors' waiting room could teach you something about love and dedication. Whether there's anything like love on the inside, I couldn't say. My guess is that it's a scarce commodity behind the walls of the high security prison in Terre Haute, Indiana, where my brother's been an inmate for the last three years after spending twenty-seven months in a Kentucky state penitentiary.

He's not much of a writer, my brother, and the truth is that I'm pretty far from comfortable with a pen and paper. The last time I sent him a letter was two years ago when our mother died of a heart attack at forty-one. I could have told him in person, but I just felt it was something better to read than to hear. Women aren't supposed to die of heart disease at that age, but mom was the type who never did a single, solitary thing in her life that might have kept her from dying young. In fact, she did just about everything she could think of to welcome that eventuality. The old man died a little over five years ago. If you're doing the math in your head right now about my father's untimely death at forty-five and how long my brother's been in prison, let me save you some trouble and say there's no coincidence.

Now if you want to talk about two human beings who deserved to be sitting in a prison cell we can sit around and discuss my parents, but some other time because today I have things to do. I have to go out to the prison on Bureau South Road to see my big brother, maybe for the last time. We can share one last talk about mom and dad although that subject rarely comes up when I'm sitting across from him in the visiting room. He likes to talk about the places he wants to see when he gets out.

I'm not behind bars, but my life hasn't been much of a picnic since I moved to this town three years ago for no other reason than to visit my brother, my only living relative. I got cousins somewhere but never met them. Kind of late in life now to think about reunions or catching up. Time to move on and put this life behind me.

I don't have a phone, and I definitely don't own a car. Not having a phone is by choice, the car is mostly a matter of not being able to afford it. The car I could afford, but the insurance would eat me alive on account of the drunk driving charge back in Kentucky. My record was expunged when I became an adult, but the insurance companies don't forget stuff like that. Not having a car is actually a blessing most of the time and most people I see around me can't afford their wheels.

I ride a bike everywhere, but I don't like to ride out to the prison. There's just something too creepy about the place so I get as close as I can and then call for a taxi. I've been coming to this dive called the 101 Bar before the last few visits, although "dive" wouldn't begin to describe the place. Unfinished plywood floors, squalid toilet, the world's rattiest pool table, and an even rattier collection of customers. If you expect something other than ratty customers at seven in the morning on a Sunday, you're setting yourself up for a major disappointment. Visiting hours at the prison begin at eight o'clock and I like to be there at eight sharp, just in case there're any snares in the visiting procedures for the day, and there almost always are.

Seven a.m. on a Sunday and the 101 has eleven customers all served by a woman who looks fifty but is probably closer to thirty. It's not like I'm a big drunk, but I have a beer just to have something to do. I sit at a table in the middle of the place. I don't want to hide in the back, but I'm not looking to make new friends. I drink slowly. I've got a bit of a wait because from here to the prison by taxi is less than ten minutes.

The 101 is open until three a.m. but then is compelled by law to close until seven a.m. Closed on Christmas, by law. Everyone in here but me looks as if they've been out all night, and lord knows where they spent those four hours when bars are supposed to be closed. I got here right at seven o'clock and the place was already up and running, so they probably shut down late and let people in early. I've seen places that just close the front door and stay open all night.

Two guys playing pool are going at it pretty good with a beer and shots. One of them is wearing a Purdue University t-shirt but if he graduated from high school, I'd buy a round for the whole bar. A ball flies off the pool table and rolls over by me under the next table. They're about as far from the stray ball as I am, but one of them grunts at me to pick it up for them.

I wasn't trying to be an asshole, but I just looked at the ball on the floor and then traced a line with my eyes towards the two pool players as if to point out the relative distance we all were from what was keeping them from their game. Then I turned my gaze away from them as if to say that I didn't give a shit about them or their ball. The truth was that I really didn't. They were both a little bigger than me, but they looked soft and tired and old for their age. One of them walked over really close to me, a bit out of his way to get the ball. At the last moment I just looked him in the eye with an attitude that said, "If you're looking for trouble, keep looking at me."

He immediately got my point and went back to his game.

At about twenty till, I called a taxi from the bar phone, paid for my drink with a decent tip, and took a piss before I left. I don't like

3

using the toilet at the prison. The two hicks playing pool made sure not to eye me when I left.

When I got to the prison and signed in, I knew immediately that something was up because there was a bit of confusion when my name was called. I stood first in line and waited as the overweight woman behind the counter talked on the phone, mostly just nodding her head. It's not like they do much ad-libbing at this place or make shit up as they go along, but she was genuinely at a loss as to what she should do for some reason. The list of rules on visitation procedures for the Federal Bureau of Prisons is seventeen pages long, so they tend to stick to the script at all times. The woman asked me about my brother's next of kin. I told her that he didn't have anyone but me. She said that they tried to phone someone last week, but there were no phone number listed on his approved list of visitors.

I asked if there was anyone else on that list besides me, but she said that was privileged information, as if a convict had some sort of right to privacy. I knew for a fact that my brother didn't have a list of visitors. He had me. He hardly knew anyone at home or in Nashville before he went in, and it's not like friends come crawling out of the woodwork once they learn you've been sentenced for murder. She told me to have a seat again and wait, which is what they say every time I come for a visit, but today something was definitely wrong. She and the other worker, another beautiful but obese woman in her 40s, went in the back and talked to someone. When they came back a few minutes later, there was a mob of people with questions and demands about their loved ones inside and the two prison employees just shot me a look as if to tell me that first they needed to avert a riot and then they'd get to me.

After about twenty minutes a man came out and called my name. He was a white guy who looked in his late thirties, but it was hard to tell because he was almost completely bald. He looked the part of prison functionary, wearing a short-sleeve light blue shirt with a cheap

4

tie. All he needed to complete the image was a pocket protector. He told me to follow him. We went behind the counter and back down a narrow hallway.

We entered an office probably the size of one of the cells, although he didn't look like the type who appreciated irony. Maybe he was proud of his little cubbyhole. He closed the door while motioning for me to have a seat in front of the metal desk where he sat.

He gave me his name and his position at the prison and after drilling me a bit on my identity and checking my state identification card, he told me that my brother was in critical condition in the prison hospital. He said there had been an "incident" last Wednesday. I wouldn't be able to visit him in the hospital for security reasons. This sounded legitimate to me, but I don't really know or care about prison rules and no one needs to tell me twice that I can't go to a hospital, which I hate more than prisons.

I asked him a bunch of questions. He didn't answer a single one and only repeated what he told me before. He told me that he could phone me with any new updates on my brother's condition. I told him about not having a phone for the third time. He gave me a number that I could call during the week and escorted me back to the waiting area.

"Good luck," he said as a way of saying goodbye.

It was 08:45 when I walked out of the prison gates. I decided to walk back to the bar to get my bicycle. I had nothing else to do and I'd save money by not taking a taxi. It only took about twenty minutes. The 101 Bar was beside railroad tracks, like almost everything else in Terre Haute. This used to be an important rail hub for parts south of Chicago, but now the tracks crisscrossing the town were like scars, an ugly reminder of something that happened a long time ago.

Trains still passed through the town, but from what I'd seen it was like they only took life away, bit by bit. I thought about that as I looked at the poorly-maintained tracks, and I couldn't recall ever seeing a passenger train pass through Terre Haute. I was the only person I'd met who came here by choice and that was only to sustain some link with my brother.

The men who came to the prison were bad news, fuck-ups even for convicts. Some of them are federal death row inmates. My brother was sent here after assaulting another inmate at the last place where he was locked up. If he messes up again, they've threatened him with an even tougher facility where he'd be locked down and alone all day, every day. From what my brother told me, nobody wants that. Nobody.

When I got close enough to the bar, I saw that my bike hadn't been stolen, which is a constant worry in small town America these days because of the tweekers. Against my better judgment I decided to have another beer inside. They say that nothing good happens after two a.m. and in the 101 Bar for all practical purposes it was still last night, meaning it was definitely after two o'clock in the morning. My two new friends were still playing pool. Of course, they were still there, what the fuck else did they have to do? Mr. Purdue University got up the alcohol courage to at least look at me.

I thought I knew his type and by himself he wouldn't look another man in the eye walking down the street. Get a night's worth of beer and whiskey in him and then drag it out into the next day and he'd become a lot less predictable. He had his little drinking buddy with him that might fool him into a sense of security adequate enough to mouth off to someone, but he'd never go the tough-guy route without back-up. I'm not always right about my instincts, but I thought I understood those two halfwits.

I swear that I don't have a chip on my shoulder. I'm not ever looking for a fight, but I learned the hard way that a man needs to be able to take care of himself in any situation. I wasn't tough enough to handle something on my own and my brother paid the price. Now we have to look at each other across a table bolted to the floor with an armed guard watching us every second. As the old joke goes, if you think my brother has it bad, you should see the other guy.

This time I sat at the bar where I could keep my back to everyone but the ugly bartender. I averted my eyes from her radiance and tried to think of nothing at all. There was nothing to gain in thinking about the past and I avoided it at all costs. The future for me never covered much ground. A paycheck down the road. Getting to work in the morning at the auto parts store five days a week, and visits to the prison Sunday morning. That had been my future since I moved to this place.

I've thought a lot about my brother, but it didn't do any good to worry about his current situation. It's not as if I could change anything. The prison official wouldn't give me any details, but I had a pretty good idea of what happened, about the "incident." It's not like inmates had accidents in prison that put them on life support. Any blanks I had about the realities of prison life my brother had been filling in for me over the years.

He took a plea agreement for second degree murder and was to serve three to five years in the state penitentiary in Kentucky. I was too young to even visit back then, but I went a couple of times with my mother. I'd sit out in the waiting area with other kids, mostly the children of inmates, a surprisingly well-behaved group for the most part. I remember how they all seemed like frightened animals ready to bolt at the slightest sign of danger, which usually meant a parent's raised hand.

Evidently, life was pretty tough in that first prison and my brother got mixed up with some bad people. He never wrote about what he did, but a few years later, when I was old enough to talk to him face-to-face, he told me that he just did what he had to do to survive, and what he did sent him to the maximum-security facility here in Terre Haute. It also put at least another five years on his sentence, five years that stipulated good behavior, which seemed highly unlikely for him at this juncture of his life.

We grew up in a small town in eastern Kentucky. A real shit hole in almost every sense of the word. Worse even than this place. It was almost all white people, mostly ignorant and racist, but that doesn't begin to explain my brother's path, this Aryan bullshit. Whatever he became in prison, well, that's on the system. My brother felt he had no other choice if he wanted to survive. Now it looked like the choice he made wasn't going to keep him alive either. I've never been a card player, but if I were, I'd never bluff. Try that with me and I'll make you show your hand. I stopped taking shit from people five years ago when I was sixteen. I finally stood up to my father. I was a skinny kid, and he was a big man, very big. He was a coward who only picked on people he knew wouldn't fight back, like my mother and her two sons. It took my brother until after he moved out to stand up to dad, but I don't think that he was ever afraid like I was.

My brother was never afraid of anything or anybody. I just think that he couldn't accept that he had to fight his own father and chose to avoid it. When I finally had enough, I ended up in the emergency room for my valor. Cops arrested my dad but nothing much came of it. He spent less time in jail than I did in the hospital. Dad's punishment would come a couple weeks after that when my brother found out and drove back from Nashville where he'd been living for the past year.

Dad took me to the baseball field near our house to shag some flies and play catch, like something resembling a real father, something he'd never really tried much before. My brother showed up at the diamond in his car. He didn't say a word, not to me and certainly not to his intended victim.

He took the bat out of my hands at home plate and chased dad around the field until he caught him running into the opposing players' dugout. With his first swing of the bat, he shattered dad's right arm. I screamed for him to stop, dad howling in pain. He hit him about four times, good shots, but nothing to the head. I don't think he was being merciful, just wanted the old man to feel every blow. Dad kept picking himself up and walking backwards.

The last swing caught him hard on the left shoulder and he staggered another step backwards falling down a long flight of concrete stairs. He was dead before the ambulance arrived.

While he was giving it to dad, he kept yelling that if he ever touched me or mom again, he was going to kill him. Growing up I could always count on my brother to keep his promises. It was two years later when I beat the living shit out of a man for the first time. It was some piece of shit my mom was seeing who came to our house drunk and started slapping her around. I told him the same thing my brother told my dad. The guy survived, but I never saw him again.

You're probably seeing what psychologists might call a "pattern of violence," something I picked up from the school therapists I had to see from time to time after dad died. But there was no pattern to it. I wasn't particularly violent, probably less so than most folks, especially in rural Kentucky where violence is a standard tool of conflict resolution. I had just decided never to take shit off of anyone ever again and hit a woman in my presence at your extreme peril.

Take my two new pals at the pool table as an example. Unless the two of them jumped me in the parking lot I wouldn't raise my hand to them, not over chicken-shit bar stuff. I've seen way too many fights over absolutely nothing. I've heard stories of guys doing serious prison time over stuff as petty as not picking a pool ball off the floor when asked. I finished my beer and gave the bartender enough to buy a round for my buddies after I left. Just thinking about how those two hicks would react to my gesture was worth the money.

I called the prison from my job at the auto parts store on Monday afternoon. They had nothing new to tell me. They asked if they could call me at this number if something came up. I told them I'd call back. I was supposed to be quitting the place on Friday, but I let my boss know that I'd stay on until he got a replacement. I could tell he was glad to keep me on, even for a bit longer.

I was going to tell my brother on Sunday that I was moving. This was something that didn't sit well at all with me, but it wasn't my idea. He told me that I needed to clear out, that things could get dangerous for me because of some shit he was mixed up with inside. I didn't understand how that affected me, but he wouldn't go into details. He backed up his request by telling me that I was wasting my life in this town, doing nothing much but visiting an older brother who was all but a lost cause. I disagreed, but I usually listened to what he had to say. I didn't have anyone else.

I had $3,400 in cash saved up. I didn't have any idea where I'd go, but I had a few ideas. I'd never been to California. I'd never been anywhere except Kentucky and now Indiana. I'd never seen the ocean, neither had my brother. I hoped he would someday. I wish that he were coming with me, but traveling alone sounded cool with me.

I bought a nice nylon backpack like you see people wearing in outdoor magazines. My plan was to pack it full of clothes and hitchhike west. I-70 passes south of town just before you get to the prison. It goes all the way to the Pacific. That would be a good start.

More than anything I wished my brother could go with me. We always talked about traveling when we were kids, but we were five years apart, which is a lot when you're young. Now that we're both

10

adults it's funny how much we have in common. I always thought that he was a lot smarter than I was, but it's not like I'm stupid. I was just younger and now I was catching up. If we just had a chance to hang out now, I was sure we'd be the best of friends. We could see the world together and watch each other's back while we did.

He even got a passport when he lived in Nashville. He showed it to me when he came home for a visit once. It just seemed like the most important document in the world. It gave you the right to go anywhere you wanted, and no one could stop you. Six months ago, I got one, too. It cost me a bit, but I didn't care. I even got a special waterproof pouch for it. You didn't need one to get to California, but from there I could head south into Mexico and then…who knows?

I called the prison again two days later. This time they put me on hold forever. Finally, a guy came on the line, said his name was Davidson and told me he was the one who spoke to me at the prison on Sunday morning. He asked me if this was my home phone. I said that it wasn't, that I didn't have a home phone. He regretted to inform me that my brother was still in intensive care. He asked for my home address just in case something came up so they could send word. This sounded a little odd to me. I told him I was moving. I'd call back with my new address. The last thing I wanted was to be in their system any more than was absolutely necessary. The truth was that his questions made me uneasy.

My place was close to where I worked, in a house that had been cut up into four apartments. "Apartment" was sort of a generous word for where I lived, which was two rooms with a small bathroom. My whole place was part of the ground floor of an old Queen Anne style home that must have been a handsome place back when this town meant something in the world. My door opened into the back yard, a feature which suited me fine. It was more private, and I could keep my curtains wide open without anyone looking in at me like an animal in a small cage. Over the past few weeks since I'd decided to listen to

11

my brother and cut out of town, I made it so everything I had fit in my backpack and threw out the rest.

It was a good feeling to have just one small bag that I could pick up and run with. It's curious because I never had much, and now that I had even less, I actually felt better, lighter—almost light enough to fly. I couldn't explain it except to say I was looking forward to traveling. It's not even like I was looking forward to seeing new places. It was more a question of never having to see the old places ever again. I wouldn't miss this dump of an apartment or this town. I knew when I left that I'd never return to my hometown in Kentucky. I didn't even go back when mom died. I don't really believe in funerals, and I'm sure funerals don't matter to the dead.

After coming home from work, I passed out on my bed with my clothes on at six o'clock or so. I slept for almost three hours, which I knew would mean I'd never get to sleep later. I got up and did some cleaning as I was getting ready to leave this place, as soon as I got word on my brother. I paid week to week with no deposit, but I still wanted to leave it clean when I left. The woman who owned the place always treated me well. At midnight I went back to bed and tried to sleep again.

Maybe an hour later I was wide awake in the dark apartment when I heard the muffled sound of glass breaking. I immediately thought about my brother's warning and jumped out of bed in my underwear. Someone had shattered one of the small panes in the door and was now trying to open it. Near my backpack I had a bamboo club about a meter long and a bit thicker than a broom handle. Bamboo is lighter than most types of wood and hard. I walked into the other room just when the door opened. I could make out two of them. They didn't have a light. I suppose they were trying to do this as stealthily as possible. It was darker inside than outside, so I had the sight advantage, at least for a bit. I saw they both had shaved heads and tattoos and my assumptions were confirmed.

12

The one who came through the door first had a flashlight in his left hand, but it was switched off. He had a huge knife in his right hand. The guy entering behind him had a shotgun pointed up and to his left. I was to their left on the other side of the door. I raised the bamboo cane high over my head.

The first guy turned on the flashlight and just as he did, I swung down as hard as I could and caught the guy with the shotgun square on the top of his head. He groaned a bit, staggered, then collapsed in a heap. The flashlight guy dropped the light and lashed out at me with the hunting knife. I could tell from his first swing he didn't know what the fuck he was doing with the knife. It may as well have been a spoon for all the harm he was going to do. I swung around like I was taking a baseball swing and caught him in the middle of the back.

He started to fall forward and then spun around and came down on his side. Before I could square up another swing with the cane, I saw that he was trying to wiggle over to the shotgun on the floor. He grabbed it by the barrel and pulled it towards him. He had it in both hands just as my next blow came down and shattered his right forearm. He howled in pain, but he still had the shotgun in both hands as he lay on the floor. I kicked him in the side of his chest as hard as I could, which was really hard. He let go of the gun and rolled on his stomach. I stepped over him and gave him a good kick in the balls, then reached over for the shotgun.

I patted down the one I just kicked in the nuts. He had a wad of bills that I lifted, but no weapon. The other guy was pretty much done from what I could see. He wasn't twitching or moving at all. His head was split pretty good. Doctors can do wonders these days with head trauma, but as I said a few times, I didn't have a phone. Maybe I'd call an ambulance when I got the chance, but first I had a few questions. I had duct tape in my pack as would any good boy from Kentucky. I used it to secure the mostly-alive Nazi and covered his mouth, too. I got dressed then took a little walk around outside just to be sure it was just the two of them and nobody waiting out in the car. I took the shot gun with me.

The rifle was a real nice one, Smith and Wesson twelve gauge semi-automatic, although they messed it all up by sawing off the barrel. You never knew with knuckleheads like these two, so just to be sure, I checked the breach to verify there was a round in the chamber, then wondered if it would even fire. They probably didn't know you were supposed to clean a gun once in a while. After standing around in the shadows for a few minutes, I didn't see anyone and went back inside.

I shut the door and turned on the light. I popped the guy in the back of the head pretty hard with the barrel of the shotgun just to get his full attention. I laid the shotgun on the table a step away and picked up the cane again.

"You wanna end up like your buddy with your brains leaking out of your ears?"

I could tell that he was scared out of his mind, but he was trying hard to put on the tough guy act. I also knew that he was hurting pretty bad with at least a couple of broken ribs. I've broken a rib before and it hurts for weeks, just about every time you breathe. I never took a kick to the nuts like he just did, so I can't speak on that.

"Do you want to die tonight? Because whether you live or die is entirely my decision at this point."

This time he grunts something, so I ripped the tape off his mouth. He let loose with a string of profanities; they weren't aimed at me directly but just out of pain.

"Quiet now, I got neighbors who work tomorrow."

He was on his side with his hands taped behind his back and his legs taped together at the knees and ankles.

14

"Look, amigo, I don't have any time here to fuck around. I'm not going to ask anything you don't want to tell me because it would probably be bullshit so just tell me this: were you going to say something before you shot me? Like give me a message from your scout leader or whoever the fuck?"

"You have no idea the people you're dealing…"

I cracked his right shin sharply with the cane, making him howl yet again. I put the tape back over his mouth.

"I definitely don't have time for you to make any threats so let's just assume that you're all a big bunch of bad motherfuckers."

I took the tape off his mouth, this time not quite so violently. I didn't want to be a dick.

"This obviously has something to do with my brother, got nothing to do with me, but not according to your fucked-up rules. Do you know what that means?"

"What?" was all he could mutter.

"It means I got nothing to lose here by killing you. In fact, the only smart move for me is to kill you. Can you think of one good reason why I shouldn't bash your head in like this one?"

He didn't answer right away so I asked him another question.

"What was his name?" I asked pointing with the cane to his partner.

"Tango," he groaned.

"I mean his real fucking name, not what the other cub scouts call him. What's his real name?"

"Patrick"

"Patrick, thank you. I think we owe him that much as he lies here dying. And what's your name?"

"Jason, my name's Jason."

"OK, Jason. Take a good look at Patrick. He may live if we call an ambulance, but that doesn't seem like a good option for me, at least not right now. Do you want to end up like Patrick?"

"No."

"Did you have something you were going to say to me?"

"No, we was just supposed to shoot ya."

I was going to ask him how they found where I lived, but the answer came to me almost immediately before I could even form the words. I put the tape back over Jason's mouth.

I found car keys in the brain-dead guy's pocket. I packed up the rest of my shit and left the two of them without saying goodbye. I thought the shotgun might come in handy for my next stop and took that with me. I figured that their crew would come clean up the mess here as they wouldn't want the cops in on their attempted homicide. I didn't really care.

I stopped the car at the first booth I saw that still had a phone book and found Mr. Davidson's address, Harold Davidson, the inmate liaison officer. I didn't know where it was exactly, but I had time.

It was a little after 4 a.m. when I found Davidson's house. I was hoping that he lived alone, but at this point it didn't matter much either way as things were already very complicated. I parked a few houses down and doubled-back behind the houses. I had the shotgun and my cane along with the duct tape and a lock-blade knife I always had with me.

I got in through the back patio door that just had a screen in it. It looked like a really nice place with expensive furniture. Maybe he was just smart with his money and got by on his prison salary, and maybe not. A more likely explanation was that he was on the Aryans' payroll at the prison and giving me up was just one more little favor. I imagined he had a weapon or two in the house; I certainly would if I worked at a prison.

It was a single level ranch style home, like all the others on the block. I made my way to the backyard. I got in through the screen door on the patio which few people bothered to lock, especially in the warmer months. I heard heavy snoring. I checked the other bedroom to make sure it was empty before entering the snorer's room through an open door. This had been too easy. He was alone in the house…except for me.

I switched on the light and yelled loudly.

"Harold, are these visiting hours?"

He was sleeping on top of the blankets in tighty-whities, of course. He saw me with the shotgun pointed right at him. I could almost hear his brain working to put this puzzle together.

"Surprise! I'm not dead."

"What are you doing here? What…"

I cut him off.

"Stop! Just shut the fuck up. Listen carefully because I won't repeat myself. You try to bullshit me for a second and I will blow a fucking hole in your chest with the twelve gauge. Understand? At this point it really doesn't matter to me."

He lay frozen on the bed.

"Understand?" I yelled.

"Yes," he answered.

"Don't talk unless you're answering my questions. Lie to me and your life ends right here and now. Got it?"

He shook his head.

"Tell me exactly what the fuck happened to my brother."

I motioned for him to move over and sit on the chair by the bed. He got up and sat down facing me.

"Your brother got on the wrong side of a power struggle with the white supremacist guys. He and another inmate killed the leader, or at least everyone thinks they did. They came back at him. He was stabbed sixteen times. He died yesterday." He paused before correcting himself, "The day before yesterday."

I guess killing one father just wasn't enough for my brother.

"So, what the fuck does all that have to do with me?" I asked.

"It's a gang thing. They call it extirpation, pulling something out…"

"I know what 'to extirpate' means," I said.

"It's where they kill a guy's entire family, everyone."

"And you gave those fucking animals the phone number at the auto parts store where I work?"

"I didn't…"

I raised the shotgun to his forehead.

"Be very fucking careful about the next words to come out of your mouth."

He dropped his head and took a few deep breaths before sobbing wildly. Choking, gasping sobs.

"I don't know what I can do. I'm terrified of them. It started back when I was a guard, and I'd do little favors for them. I thought they'd treat me better, more respectfully. They started paying me a little and then…"

He stopped and broke down again.

"They've come in my house just like you're here right now, threatening to kill me and my family, my mother and father and sisters. They told me even if I quit my job, they'd kill us. If I killed myself, they'd still kill my family. What the fuck do I do?"

Even though he almost got me killed I felt sorry for this pathetic wreck of a human being. I couldn't imagine ever being such a gutless punk who's probably been pushed around his entire life. Then I thought about my own character and how I'd paid a pretty heavy price so that I wouldn't take shit anymore, but I was still alive after everything that happened tonight. Maybe my life was a mess right now, but I thought that I was better off than this poor slob. I'm usually not in the advice-giving business, but this guy desperately needed it.

"Sooner or later this human filth you're working for will kill you and maybe your whole family as they've threatened. I'd say that you need to stop what you're doing no matter the consequences. They could've killed me tonight. Tomorrow maybe it'll be someone else because of you, an innocent person just like your family."

He didn't even look up at me.

"From what I saw tonight these guys aren't exactly the fucking A-Team. Understand? You need to come down on them. You still have power over them. Use it."

I looked at him and reconsidered.

"Or just fucking quit. I'm guessing they'd forget all about you and work on the next guy."

I got $358 off the two guys who tried to kill me and another $735 from the prison officer. Not much, but every little bit helps. It was a shame to have to throw the shotgun away, but guns were nothing but trouble, especially a completely illegal sawed-off that was probably stolen. I drove the would-be killers' car for about three hours west on I-70 until it got low on gas. I pulled off on an exit ramp, ditched the car as best I could, and hitchhiked from there.

My first time hitchhiking and it's going well. No one knows me and I can be anyone I want to be. I've only been on the road for three days and I may make it to the coast by tomorrow, but there's no hurry. My past is behind me and that's enough for now.

DEEP IN THE COUNT

The cop waddled toward him, palming the service weapon on his hip.

"License and registration."

The car was clean. He made sure, even double-checked the taillights before leaving. He wasn't speeding, not with the contents in the trunk. He was a professional.

"I do something wrong, officer?"

Breathing heavily from his walk from the cruiser, he didn't condescend to answer the driver's question.

Probably nothing, but if things broke the wrong way, a tiny .380 auto was within easy reach. Although he wasn't at all, he tried to sound nervous, thinking that would be a normal person's reaction.

"Just driving home, listening to the ballgame."

He'd lowered the volume, but it was loud enough to hear that O'Keefe fouled off his eleventh pitch in the bottom of the ninth, down by a run and a man on base. Whatever this tub of guts wanted, he picked a bad time to do it with Seattle on the verge of a wild card spot in the playoffs…and the trunk.

"How much ya had to drink?"

"Don't drink."

He did, of course, but not tonight. He wasn't about to walk into a loaded question on a par with, "Have you stopped beating your wife?"

Another foul. Was that twelve, thirteen?

"Care to step out of the vehicle, do a few standardized sobriety tests?"

He definitely didn't care to get out of the car which was another step in this bullshit traffic stop heading way south. He didn't want to refuse flat out, not this soon which would only get this hick cop's gander up even more.

Never get out of the car; everyone knew that.

Another foul to left.

"Sir, I need you to exit of the vehicle."

Vehicle? Who used that term except moron small-town cops trying to sound like they actually graduated from high school? He shot a casual leftward glance. The cop's huge gut was spilling over his utility belt, practically covering the handle of his revolver. It looked about as comfortable as being wrapped in barbed wire. The cop had zero for probable cause, but who cared. Anything police invented was difficult to dispute in court, especially if they found evidence of a capital crime in the trunk.

"Did'ya hear me? Said outta the damn vehicle."

The mild profanity was unfortunate. An escalation. He needed to calm things down or this could be fat boy's last shift—an unnecessary complication to what should've been a routine disposal.

"Not asking again," now shouting.

He leaned over and turned up the radio.

"Keep your hands where I can see'em," his movement putting the cop in full-blown panic mode.

"Sorry, but O'Keefe just fouled off his seventeenth pitch," he said. "Seattle down by one in the bottom of the ninth, Hummel on base. Two outs!"

The cop said nothing, so he turned the radio up again. People in these mountain towns east of Seattle were either baseball fans or they hated the game and only followed football.

"O'Keefe's on fire lately."

OK, maybe this didn't have to end in a bloodbath, he thought. He likes baseball.

"How many's that?"

"Nineteen."

"Damn, must be a record, right?" the cop asked.

"Brandon Belt, 2018. Twenty-one pitches. Oakland's pitcher hasn't thrown a single ball."

"Damn!" the cop gasped.

This epic at-bat could go on way too long. If back-up happened by, it'd seriously complicate a situation that was already problematic.

"Twenty! How in the hell can anyone hit twenty fouls?" the astonished cop asked.

A dull thud came from the back of the car, but the cop was talking, waiting on the next pitch tying the record.

Foul.

"What a great player," the cop said.

Another kick from the trunk. What the fuck? Then he heard gagging. Alive? How? A disgraceful rookie mistake.

"This's it," the cop squealed.

The trunk distraction made him forget about the game, but the cop hadn't.

"Twenty-two pitches! A new record!"

More volume.

"Jesus, another foul! Twenty-three!"

Another death rattle was muted by the radio announcer screaming about a home run.

Seattle wins.

"Glad I pulled you over to hear that," the cop said. "Sometimes you just get lucky."

You've no idea how lucky you were tonight, officer, he thought.

BETTING MAN'S JUDGEMENT DAY

He didn't think when he woke up late on Monday that it'd be his last day on this earth, but after seven phone calls from six different pissed-off people, he had a pretty good idea of it by lunchtime. Monday, as in the day after Sunday, as in play-off Sunday. Not Cal's lucky day, to put it as politely as human speech could describe it.

Cal had already been celebrating what he thought would be the biggest payday of his life when the Steelers made a safety with thirty seconds on the clock. Two minutes earlier, Miami had kicked a field goal to cover his spread. A safety? It was like the worst practical joke in history.

"Imagine losing by a safety with half a minute to go, that's like getting struck by lightning after walking away from a plane crash," some numb-nuts at the bar said when the whistle blew.

Cal punched him in the stomach, even though it was a good line, something he'd probably use. He got the hell out of there, didn't even bother paying his bill. The last thing Cal needed was an assault charge tacked on to this catastrophe, although the county jail seemed safe and secure to him right at that moment.

"Anger issues much?" a waitress snarled at him after he laid the guy out on the floor.

Cal hated that tired-ass verbal tick, the thing about adding "much" after damn near anything, something that passed for wit these days. He felt like knocking a few of her teeth out, but he needed to get the hell out of there before the cops showed up.

In defiance of his morbid hangover, Cal managed to pull it together enough to get dressed. He always gave himself credit for thinking fast. After his second cup of coffee, he was out the door with a plan in his throbbing head. There was just no way he could avoid the McCollough brothers, but he had a few stops to make along the way to bolster his odds.

It's difficult to discern another man's real intentions while he's screaming an aria of obscenities at you on the other end of a phone call, as was the case this morning in his talk with the older McCollough brother, Warren.

As he drove down the narrow gravel road towards the McCollough farm, he wouldn't have taken any bets on his chances of driving back the opposite way after he met with the three brothers to face the music. He didn't see any other way around his quandary at this point, with "quandary" being Warren's word for the money he owed. And then there were his other transgressions.

The money part he could just run away from. They'd try to find him, but it's not like the McCollough's have the money or resources to hunt a man down like Osama Bin Laden. Even if they found him, they'd just drag his sorry ass back and find a way for him to make good on what he owed them, maybe even let him throw down something on a game if he was behaving himself. If he won, they'd take it off his tab. But Cal lost most of the time. That probably goes without saying.

See, Cal liked to think of everything in terms of the odds. He could figure the probabilities on damn near anything, or at least he thought he could. He was good with numbers and could make calculations in his head, no paper or calculator necessary He knew more than anyone about professional football, at least anyone in those parts. He actually read about football, and not just the newspapers, but books.

Obviously, someone, somewhere knew more about the game because Cal lost a lot more than he won, like gamblers of any stripe. They'd let you know when they won alright, wouldn't shut up about it. Never heard a peep out of them about the losses, unless to say how they got robbed by a bad call or some other puerile bullshit, like their excuses mattered to whoever took their money.

Which was why he was in the situation he found himself in now, driving slowly down a three-quarter-mile gravel road to meet his fate. A hundred to one Cal gave himself, a hundred to one he'd be driving back the other direction when this was settled. Driving home was the winning pot. Losing? Broken bones, or a mouthful of smashed teeth? Eaten by famished pigs? Buried out in the woods somewhere?

No one got killed over gambling debts, that was movie bullshit. In movies, folks can afford to kill their bread and butter. Killing a degenerate gambler because he owes you money is like a tick killing its host. Makes no sense. It wasn't that Cal didn't owe the McColloughs a lot of money, he owed then plenty, but they were thinking of killing him because he was making them look bad by taking action anywhere he could find it while in to them for everything he had, and then some.

The McColloughs hadn't let Cal put a nickel on either of Sunday's two play-off games. But word gets around, something Cal should have known better than anyone. When they found out early Monday morning that Cal had laid down big on Miami with another bookie, and that he came up one single point shy, their patience with him had vanished as quickly as Cal's pre-safety euphoria.

He could see the house way up ahead and then he saw Duane closer to him, about fifty yards or so down the drive carrying a shovel for some damn reason. Did he plan on burying Cal right out front? With Duane by himself so far from the house, Cal upped his odds now to about twenty to one.

Cal rolled to a stop ten yards in front of Duane and his shovel. Cal considered that distance, ten yards. If he made it forward from here, he'd have a first down, new life, a second chance.

"No need for the shovel, Duane, I come bearing gifts," Cal said out the window.

Duane chuckled and moved forward to Cal's sedan. Cal gripped the pole sitting on the passenger seat. Duane walked up and put his hands on the door of Cal's open driver side window and bent over a bit.

"You got a speargun?" Duane asked, puzzled.

His expression and posture changed quickly, but not fast enough to dodge the harpoon that tore into his chest. He fell on his back and pulled futilely with both hands on the object piercing his heart.

Cal *didn't* have a speargun, at least not until an hour ago. He wanted a silencer for a pistol, but those are tough to get on short notice. Walmart sells spearguns, as it turns out.

"I never fucking liked you, Duane," Cal said out loud to the harpooned hillbilly.

He didn't mean for it to be funny or pithy, like those stupid lines in movies that are supposed to sound ominous, like, "*Hasta la luego*, baby," but he thoroughly disliked Duane McCollough, always had. The "harpooned hillbilly" bit, which he'd thought to himself, was a little funny. He liked a good laugh as much as the next guy, but he had a lot to do, and they were called Arnold and Warren, Duane's two surviving elder siblings.

Cal got out of the car and grabbed Duane by his ankles and dragged him a couple yards away, ditching the body in some bushes. Cal thought of it as a body, as in corpse, but Duane was still making a bit of noise. The guy was as good as dead, it's just that Cal didn't have time to tell him.

He drove up to the house and parked. Left his keys in the ignition so as to have one less thing to worry about if he had to leave in a hurry, which he figured at about ninety-nine percent likely. Before he closed his car door, he revised those chances to one hundred percent as he couldn't imagine a single scenario in which he left this place in anything less than a panic.

There were three vehicles at the house belonging to the brothers, so maybe that meant there wasn't anyone else here but Arnold and Warren. Cal raised his odds of getting out of this to ten to one.

The McCollough place had been in their family since it was built in 1889 and was as handsome as it'd ever been. The parents had died several years ago, and the three brothers all lived there now. Sort of an unhealthy situation, in Cal's mind. None of them ever married and Cal had never seen any of them with women, at least not for a while. It was their business, creepy, but their damn business.

Cal walked up the stairs to the porch carrying Duane's shovel. He leaned it next to the big oak door, rapped the brass knocker, and waited. Took over a minute for an answer, but the house was sprawling, and Cal wasn't in a hurry for what was coming next. Arnold opened the door.

"You know the drill, Cal," he said.

Cal knew the drill and turned his back to Arnold and raised his hands over his head. Arnold patted him down thoroughly. No one saw Warren without a search.

Cal's original plan was to use the speargun at the door on whoever answered. The speargun turned out to be a stroke of genius, but now he was already into his improvised Plan B on account he only had one harpoon.

"Why the hell did Duane leave the shovel here?" Arnold said, just noticing the tool leaning against the house beside the door as he walked into the foyer.

Cal walked in behind him, picking up the shovel.

Arnold led him into the dining room and told him to take a seat, make himself at home. Cal thought that was a nice thing to say, especially considering what a huge deadbeat he was these days. He used to hang out quite a bit with Arnold, back before Arnold quit drinking and gambling. After that, they had nothing in common.

Cal liked this middle brother. He felt warm thinking about the power of friendship and was glad that Arnold wasn't the one lying out in the bushes with a harpoon in his heart.

Arnold hollered from the dining room doorway and up the stairs for his older brother. As soon as he finished and before he could turn around again, Cal smashed his head in with the shovel. Arnold fell in a heap, just twitching a bit while making a low noise like air leaking out of a beachball. Cal thought about hitting him again just to be on the safe side, but he looked pretty damn dead. Cal dragged the middle brother into the big walk-in closet in the hallway and closed the door.

Cal sat down at the dining room table with ten chairs. He knew better than to sit at the head of the table, not when he was going to talk to Warren. That spot was his. Should've called himself Prince Warren, the egomaniacal prick.

Cal never understood how Warren thought he was so high and mighty when all he did was inherit what his family handed to him on a platter. Arnold and Duane were even more useless, at least in Cal's estimation, but at least Arnold wasn't so uppity about being a McCollough. Duane was the muscle of the family, or at least he used to be because he hadn't dirtied his own hands in forever. That didn't keep him from being an arrogant jerk who thought he was a real tough guy.

As Cal sat in the rather majestic antique dining room, he savored the fact that he had the last laugh with Duane. Cal was better with numbers than with words and thought that "last laugh" probably wasn't the correct way to describe his final encounter with the youngest McCollough brother.

This got Cal thinking about those last words, words that Duane was too busy dying to hear, probably.

I never fucking liked you, Duane.

A couple dozen other lines went through his mind of what he could have said. Of course, it was too late now, but that didn't mean he couldn't embellish the story with something clever and more poignant. Poor Arnold didn't even get a last line from him. This wasn't the time and place to make aesthetic improvements on his final words with Duane, who wasn't exactly Cal's nemesis like the bad guys in movies.

The truth was that they'd hung out quite a bit, too, maybe more than he did with Arnold. Now that he thought about it, he and Duane had some pretty wild times together. He'd known him his entire life. They played football together from pee-wee until high school. Duane was a wide receiver with Cal at quarterback. Granted, they were a running team, but he and Duane pulled off some magic from time to time. Everyone ran back then, just the way it was. It wasn't Cal's fault that Duane hardly touched the ball.

Arnold was the same year as Cal and played a bit. Left tackle, but he never had the heart for the game.

Warren was three years older, so Duane, Arnold, and Cal never played with him. A true legend at running back. Didn't have the size to play college, but he broke a few records in high school.

Where the hell was he?

Cal scanned the dining rooms for possible weapons. He'd read a novel way back about an assassin who could kill with only a pencil.

31

No damn pencils that he could see. He'd prefer a sawed-off 12-gauge. He'd open up with both barrels the moment Warren stepped into sight.

He heard someone walking down the stairs. Finally. Warren entered the dining rooms through the full-sized swinging doors, right where his kid brother got his head dented.

Cal started to stand up, but Warren motioned for him to keep his seat.

"First of all, I want to apologize for my behavior on the phone earlier," Warren said.

Damn, Cal thought. When he talks like that, I don't hate him too much,

Warren went on to talk about the game on Sunday and how that was just a tragic screw up by the Dolphins, not that it mattered for their play-off hopes as the game was over long before their quarterback inexplicably wandered into his own end zone and was hit so hard by a Steelers' defender that he had to be taken off the field on a stretcher.

He sounded almost consoling. He wasn't tickled that Cal had bet big with another bookie on the game, but he thought they could work things out.

"I like you, Cal."

Cal was flattered beyond words. Warren McCollough likes me, he thought.

"You know I'm good for it, Warren. I'm not going anywhere."

Warren stood up and gave Cal a hug. A hug!

"It's all good, Cal."

Cal hated that expression, but not this time.

"It's only money, after all, and you're almost like family around here.

Not exactly what Cal had anticipated for his tête-à-tête with the head of the McCollough clan.

"Talk to Duane before you leave, he's out there digging up some of the winter crop potatoes for you. We got loads of them this year."

"Thanks, Warren.

Cal stepped off the porch and walked to his car.

Cal was way off on his odds for being in a hurry while leaving the McCollough house. He couldn't have been in less of a hurry. In fact, he didn't want to leave, still basking in the glow of Warren's approbation. Being in an absolute state of shock will do that to a guy. Then he thought about Warren maybe needing something from the closet. Better get his ass in gear.

He drove down the gravel drive and looked over at the bushes where Duane had passed his final moments. Cal considered removing the harpoon from his chest. The speargun was expensive, he'd only used it once, and Walmart had an excellent return policy.

He reminded himself that he didn't have time. He had another extremely angry bookie to confront, and there were probably several firearms in that same closet where Warren was going to find his brother sooner or later.

Cal put his odds at fifty-fifty.

EARLY RELEASE

The first time I set foot in this penitentiary I was overwhelmed by the ghastly smell and the noise. Piss, sweat, and the constant din of shouting are difficult things to come to terms with, but worse is knowing the system is a complete and utter failure. After more than twenty years in this place, I've witnessed few success stories. No one would've included me among those fortunate few who left and never returned, the rehabilitated and the free at last, but I finally have an escape plan.

Like almost everyone else trapped behind these walls and bars, I never dreamed I'd be here this long. Like so many other pathetic cases inside, one mistake led to another, one bad life choice seemed to heap three more on top of it, like a pile-up car accident. Before you know it, you're doing twenty to life. I watched too many people die before they could move on. Years ago, I thought I could walk away, have some completely different life. Happy was something I was never able to imagine, but I thought I had it in me to conjure up a different world, a place without locks, barbed wire, and the constant threat of brutality.

What crime sentenced me to this purgatory? I'm guilty of the sin of my birth. I was born in this godforsaken town. Most prisons are in places where manufacturing fled like a thief in the middle of the night decades ago, leaving few jobs above minimum wage. Being a prison guard is the modern equivalent of working in the mines. If you're from some forgotten backwater in Appalachia, you go down a hole in the ground. Here, you go behind bars. No light enters either place.

It pays well, especially in these rust-belt archipelagos where prices were frozen when the unions died off a generation ago. The problem is the soul-crushing nature of watching over the human detritus entombed in our criminal justice system.

I ended up here after flunking out my first semester at the state university. I thought of joining the military, but my girlfriend was pregnant and wanted me around. Didn't know what I wanted back then, but it wasn't the "daddy prison hack" version of a life, but with nothing better on the horizon, I signed up and began on the night shift. On my first training shift, the smell and noise almost sent me packing.

Just a temporary gig, right? I'd move on, find a better job, but life got in the way: three kids, orthodontics, private Catholic schools, a mortgage, and car payments held me in this place like a sentence without the possibility of parole. Now I'm coming up on enough time to retire at half pay, but if I stay another seven years, I can get seventy-five percent. And like a convict who just can't go straight, I was ready to stay on, collect a full three quarters pension for the rest of my life. It's only seven more years, I told myself. Easy time.

Seven more years dealing with the total wretchedness of this place, the hellish racket of constant screaming, yelling, threats, profanity, the petty arguments of uneducated guards and convicts, the claustrophobia of locked doors and gates crashing shut, the insane alarms pounding in your ears, and the devastating violence as ever-present as the foul air. Seven more years, then I can move on, learn to paint, or play the piano. Of course, I could've done those things years ago, but I never knew how or where to start. I was scared to death of leaving this place, for something, anything new. Finally, I'm more horrified of staying than forging into the unknown.

I can thank my youngest son for my change of heart, my sudden act of courage, my decision to retire in three months and never look back. Hank's a great kid, but not much of a student like his older siblings, both doing well at college. Hank's a junior in high school, graduates next year. One question from Hank and I decided we needed to pack up and leave this town immediately.

"Dad, can you get me a job at the prison?"

PRIMOS

The Chinese military strategist Sun Tzu wrote extensively on the art of deception in warfare. Pastor had never read the 2,500-year-old treatise, but he'd seen someone in a movie talk about it. Maybe some dead guy from China had written a book on the subject, Pastor thought, but the gypsies could teach the old master volumes on deception. Misdirection, prevarication, and fraud had been integral tools in the survival of his people in Europe for over half a millennium.

Born and raised in Valencia, Spain, Pastor still spoke with hints of the deep southern Andalusian accent of his parents who hailed from a gypsy clan from Cadiz, the south of the south. He'd attended school—practically at government gunpoint and very briefly—so he was able to read and write, an achievement his parents and grandparents had never reached. He was a clever kid. His teachers had begged the boy to apply himself. He always had issues of truancy, and at thirteen, the police stopped coming around to bring him back. Finally, he was able to dedicate himself to his chosen career.

The more fashionable term for Pastor's people was Rom, or Roma, but he was proud to call himself a gypsy, or *gitano* in Spanish. The word came from "Egypt" as it was once thought that his people came to the Iberian Peninsula via North Africa.

Few people can claim at thirty-two that they've put in over twenty years on the job, but Pastor had been born and bred for his profession. Had he applied himself at school and then in some other career, who knows how much he could have achieved, but he never considered any other life. Everything else, all those other choices, were the thing of *payos*, the gypsy word for non-gypsy. Pastor knew *payos*, he did business with them, he even shared drinks with non-gypsies on occasion, but never in his life had he ever considered—even for a moment—following their incomprehensible lifestyle.

Working a job for someone else, someone not related to you? Punching a clock? Wearing some sort of absurd uniform, maybe even a tie? *¡Joder!* He would've shuddered at the thought of it, except he never thought of it. Ever. Not even once. Why would he? He was born into something completely different. *Payos* were fools who worked, paid taxes they didn't have to pay. *Payos* lived with rules governing every aspect of their sorry existence.

Of course, the life path of Pastor had been intersected on many occasions by the law enforcement authorities of the *payos*. He'd been arrested a number of times, too many to count. Spain was rather tolerant of non-violent crime. Pastor had only spent two years in prison for his dozens of convictions. Prison for a Spanish gypsy was like going to a business retreat. He met members of other clans, drank and smoked slightly less than normal, and actually exercised a bit. He walked out of the gate of the prison in Picassent like a recent graduate with an advanced business degree.

Pastor hit the pavement running like a racehorse. He had new ideas, better angles, more ambitious plans for his future. He made the decision to scrap collecting scrap, to steal away from stealing. He was moving into a world where there was real money: drugs.

Marijuana didn't seem to be worth the effort, at least that's what Pastor heard from his people in the Picassent lock-up. These days, people could grow pot legally on the balconies of their apartments. Granted, it was shit weed, but this lowered the price while also lowering demand. Cocaine was more profitable to move and less cumbersome to transport.

Only two days after he walked out of prison, Pastor was driving a new-ish panel van, compliments of his clan. The gift wasn't out of benevolence, that's not how the clan worked. They expected immediate returns on their investment. They had plans for him.

Pastor picked up his first delivery of cocaine from Malaga a week later.

They started him off small with one kilo packed into his van full of boxes of shoes he'd picked up along the way in Murcia. There was no exchange of cash at the points where the drugs were handed over. The gypsies didn't trust each other any more than they trusted the non-gypsies, but Pastor was working with family on this consignment, and they knew where he lived. Pastor knew that even if he were arrested and the dope was confiscated, his cousins would still demand payment.

They made this point abundantly clear to him before he set off from Malaga, so clearly that Pastor decided that he was probably in the wrong business. When your own family threatens to beat you to death over non-payment of a debt, he felt he was in over his head. He never complained about his income from his other hustles which never warranted violence or threats. In addition to the possibilities of incurring bodily harm, prison time for drugs wouldn't be a vacation.

He'd never thought much about the meaning of family in a gypsy clan. He called the four men he'd dealt with in Malaga cousins, but he'd never seen two of them in his life. Cousin—*primo* in Spanish—was a vague term among gypsies, and while they may share traces of DNA, he'd have a hard time making a direct familial link to any of them, let alone have their phone numbers.

He found a buyer for the complete bundle only days after returning to Valencia. He could have broken down the package and cut it up to make four or five times more, but he just wanted enough to pay off his debt and give himself something for the effort. He wanted out of the drug business. He wasn't so stupid to announce this to anyone, he just knew that he wouldn't make other moves for his Malaga cousins, and that would be that.

One of his Malaga *primos*, the one he met only that one time, the one they called e*l Oso*, the bear, the nastiest, most threatening of the four, had other plans for Pastor.

El Oso called him two weeks after Pastor paid off his cousins for the consignment. He told Pastor he had another shipment lined up for him, bigger this time, more money he promised. Pastor had a story already made up about how busy he would be and didn't have time to make the drive down and back to the south.

"You work for me now, *primo*," El Oso said.

By nature, non-confrontational, Pastor didn't want to argue on the phone. He listened to what Oso had to say while saying as little as possible before ending the conversation without making any commitments.

I work for you? Pastor thought. Like hell I do. If I wanted a job, I'd deliver mail. As big and threatening and well-connected as his cousin may have been, Pastor had never been good about dealing with authority. At school, they said he didn't respect authority. He had no respect for his putative cousin the second he had laid out the repercussions Pastor would face if he didn't pay off his debt on his first drug deal with *el Oso*. It wasn't that he disrespected his cousin before. He simply had no respect for him, which was different. Now he thought of him as an adversary.

Like many clans, Pastor's people worked on something along the lines of a generational pyramid scheme in which clan members paid up percentages of their earnings to those above them with the hope and expectation of one day receiving the same tribute when their time came to rise. The patriarch in Pastor's clan was a sixty-four-year-old who until only a year earlier had ruled from his prison cell in Picassent.

He called himself Winston, after Winston Churchill. He would have preferred Churchill as his nickname, but that was too difficult for most Spanish to pronounce, while most could manage Winston because they were familiar with the cigarette. He lived in an abandoned country mansion where he squatted after his release. Spanish law made it almost impossible for police to evict anyone once they moved into a dwelling, and no one seemed too worried that the old man was squatting in the half-ruined farmhouse, or *masia* as they are called in the Valencia countryside. Not only was Winston living rent-free, but he'd rigged a powerline to live on bootleg electricity. He had no running water and cooked on a butane-bottle stove. He was completely off the grid, like a true gypsy.

Only a year after claiming the house as his own, Winston had filled what had been an elegant garden with the detritus of his scrap metal and junk empire, turning what had been a picturesque, abandoned country manor into a squalid eyesore. The local constable unable to evict the old man, had warned Winston that if he didn't clear away the debris, they'd level the entire structure. Winston never responded to these threats; he had dozens of other squats in mind.

He had over two hundred local people paying up to him on a regular basis. Just how often and how much amounted to something of a mystery, or at least a very well-kept secret. Gypsies weren't fond of the time structure of the *payos*; years, months, days, and smaller units meant almost nothing to them. People paid their tribute to the patriarch when they could, but not paying at all was as unthinkable as taking a day job for members of the clan.

Pastor drove out to the patriarch's squat which was just minutes outside the city limits yet seemed to be in the middle of nowhere. Pastor had met Winston while in lock-up and the two became close friends. He'd taught the old guy to play chess, and they played together often, two bad players more interested in drinking and smoking cigars than what was happening on the board—perhaps the best way to approach the game. The old man always won. Pastor made sure of it, sometimes going to grand, creative lengths to ensure this outcome. Pastor had made losing to Winston something of an art in the game of kings.

Pastor thought that one day, he could be the patriarch. If he made it that far, no one would have to let him win a game, not in chess, not in anything.

Pastor called Winston "*Pere*" when he addressed him, from the local dialect meaning father, a language he only learned in prison even though most of the folks in his *barrio* of Cabanyal spoke Valenciano more than Spanish, preferring even to write the name of their neighborhood in dialect instead of using the Spanish spelling of Cabañal. The prison in Picassent naturally, hired many of the guards from the neighboring village where Valenciano was spoken almost exclusively. To gain favor with their overseers, prisoners often spoke in the local dialect.

The old man's house really was something, or it could have been with a little hard work. As shabby as the exterior looked, inside was extremely neat and tidy, something of a gypsy trait. The structure was well over one hundred-fifty years old, yet all of the wooden window shutters worked, and the doors were sturdy enough to keep out an army. There was a life-sized brass fist on the front door that served as a knocker. Pastor gave it one hard wrap.

"*Pere*, I apologize for not coming to see you sooner. I've been busy and I want to pass some of my good fortune on to you." Pastor said.

"You're a good boy, Pastor, but you don't need to give me money to come by for a chat and a game," Winston said.

As is the case in well over three hundred days a year in Valencia, it was sunny and warm. The old man led Pastor to the back terrace of ceramic tiles shaded by an untended olive tree. A small table with two folding chairs paid tribute to a chess board with a game in progress frozen in time. Pastor took a seat in front of black.

"We can start over," *Pere* offered.

"Let's finish this game on the board."

Pastor with black was already down several key pieces which only meant it would be less difficult for him to lose. He usually had to play extremely carefully to ensure that the old man won in spite of the patriarch's shallow grasp of the intricacies of the game. Pastor found that a well disguised loss could be both satisfying and relaxing. The truth was that he hated the highly competitive, confrontational aspect of chess. When there was nothing at stake, winning didn't matter to Pastor, and he didn't think enough of his skills to play for money.

During their game, Pastor talked about his recent problems with his cousin, *el Oso*, from Malaga. He never expected favors from the leader of his clan, and he doubted that *Pere* could help him with this predicament, he was simply making conversation. *Pere* had done business with *el Oso* in the past and had scant advice for his chess opponent.

"Be careful with that one. He's a snake, and the best way to deal with a viper is to avoid it."

Valencia and Malaga were separated by over six hundred kilometers, or more than six driving hours. It wasn't a problem to keep away from his cousin. *Oso* phoned him several times, but Pastor had an annoying habit of talking nonsense instead of disagreeing with someone. His cousin assumed that the Valenciano wasn't the sharpest tool in the shed.

The thing with families, and gypsy families in particular, is that you can never avoid a relative for very long. Even the most distant of cousins were sure to meet at a wedding, first communion, baptism, or funeral of a shared relative.

The clans weren't particularly religious, but they took baptisms very seriously. On this afternoon on the outskirts of Murcia, almost equidistant between Valencia and Malaga, the local patriarch was celebrating his grandson's christening. There were over one hundred vehicles parked on a dirt field next to the patriarch's farmhouse, with several hundred people in attendance from all over Spain and Portugal.

There was enough food and alcohol for at least a thousand guests, or at least normal guests, so the patriarch had planned perfectly to accommodate a couple hundred Roma who ate and drank more than those normal fools. Food, music, drinking, dancing, gossiping, and gambling burned like forest fires through every acre of the party grounds. Pastor didn't expect to see his cousin, but he wasn't surprised in the least when Oso came up to him from behind and slapped him on the shoulder.

"*Hola, primo*," Oso shouted.

Pastor was actually glad to see him, although his cheer was partly the result of the Johnnie Walker Blue he'd been drinking with a group of musicians. He could strum a few flamenco chords on a guitar, but the whiskey robbed him of whatever skill he had. He leaned on his guitar for support and was singing along with the chorus and clapping rhythmically to the odd timing of the music.

Pastor hugged his primo. They clinked glasses.

Pastor thought that Oso, in his expensive suit and shoes, looked like a mafia don. Oso may have looked the part, but he was no Pablo Escobar or *el Chapo*. He was a wealthy man within the circle of the group gathered on that day in Murcia, but Oso was a glorified middleman for *narcotraficantes* from Mexico. He didn't have an army of sicarios, or hitmen who enforced his rule and spread his empire throughout Europe.

Pastor thought little of Oso. He was a bully who was trying to force his distant cousin into the dangerous and highly risky world of cocaine sales. Pastor had risked going to jail for fifteen years on his cocaine run from Malaga and had made a couple thousand euros. He could make that selling a few stolen kitchen appliances. No one went to jail over refrigerators or stoves.

"*Primo*, we need to talk," Oso said standing over Pastor with his shoulders squared in an effort to project strength and malice.

It was sort of an unwritten rule among gypsies that you weren't supposed to conduct business at these festivities. All gypsy rules were unwritten, and in their hundreds of years of existence throughout the world, very little about them had ever been committed to paper, almost none of it written by the Roma people. A good percentage of them were illiterate.

"Gypsy rule" was an oxymoron if ever there was one, and not following rules was probably at the top of their list of unwritten rules. This summons seemed to Pastor like nothing he'd ever accepted or cared to accept, no matter the pay day. Pastor was doing his best to think a few moves ahead of this vague family member trying to force him into some sort of contract no gypsy would ever accept.

Pastor followed Oso into the vast sea of parked vehicles until they stopped beside a new black Dodge Charger. American muscle cars were very in vogue, and this monster was at the top of the heap. Pastor evidently hadn't received the memo on the topic because he showed no sign he was impressed by his cousin's menacing new set of wheels.

"Seven hundred horsepower. The fastest car on the planet," Oso said to Pastor.

The prideful owner waited for Pastor to respond.

Pastor played dumb and stood with a look on his face like he'd never seen an internally-combusted vehicle before. He scratched his head as if in deep thought before giving his opinion.

"That's a lot of horsepower. As a gypsy, perhaps you should have bought one with donkey power."

Oso didn't have much of an aptitude for humor.

"What?"

"Are we out here just to look at your car?" Pastor asked.

Oso was irritated that Pastor had compounded the insult of the comment he didn't understand with this impatient question.

"You haven't been answering your phone. We have business to do."

Pastor was prepared for this. He knew that Oso wasn't going to simply let him walk away, he had a new car to pay off, while Pastor had paid off the panel van only months after he received it after being released from prison. Pastor looked at the American race car and thought that it violated yet another law in the unwritten gypsy code: don't draw attention to yourself, especially police attention.

He wouldn't even ride as a passenger in this ridiculous vehicle for fear of getting stopped by some bored *Guardia Civil* agent who could spot a gypsy at 130 kilometers per hour. Pastor drove his van like he was still in a driver's education class because he was almost always up to no good. There was almost always something in the back he wouldn't care to have a cop inspect very carefully, and although he wasn't a drunk, he liked to have a few beers with lunch with the obligation to drive home.

Oso hadn't threatened him. Oso wasn't very clever, but he knew better than to push too hard against someone from another clan. Heavy-handed tactics usually ended badly for *payos* trying to lean on gypsies, and gypsies also didn't particularly care for anyone of their kind being too forceful. If they allowed anyone to strong-arm them, they may as well just give up and punch a clock like all the other suckers out there in the world.

Pastor thought that Oso was one of those types who just couldn't take "no" for an answer, but he didn't want to tell him to fuck off. He'd learned in prison that you never knew when someone you thought was an adversary could become a useful asset, and vice versa. Even if he could never bring himself to see eye to eye with his cousin, Pastor wanted to give the impression that he knew Oso was a few steps above him in the pecking order. One of Pastor's great strengths was the way he steered others to underestimate him, like playing a queen down on the board, a tactic he mastered playing the old man.

Pastor went into his routine of talking nonsense without ever saying that he wouldn't do what Oso was asking. He mentioned a host of problems with his wife and two children and how he was busy talking care of the clan patriarch who was getting on in years.

"Are you with me on this or not?" Oso demanded.

"*Sí, sí, sí, primo,*" Pastor said, almost shouting. "Of course, I'm looking forward to it."

However, he made it clear that he needed to get back to the party and that they could work out what his next move would be on another day. Pastor left his cousin with the joke that the next day wouldn't be a good time either because of the hangover he anticipated.

"Let's have a drink together at the party."

Pastor offered this suggestion as a way to end their meeting, having no intention of spending another moment with his distant cousin, not at this baptism nor anywhere else if he could work it. He knew that extricating himself from his new business partner was going to involve more than simply ignoring Oso's phone calls. Their parting of ways would have to appear to be his cousin's idea and was going to be considerably more complicated than allowing *Pere* to beat him at chess, but similar in tactics.

Oso had something else to say before Pastor could slip back to the party. He held Pastor by both shoulders.

"Just remember to keep your fucking mouth shut about anything we do together," he said.

Pastor wasn't surprised by the threatening tone of his cousin. He definitely wasn't afraid. He'd sized him up from their first meeting in Malaga. Pastor referred to these types as peacocks. They made a lot of noise, took up a lot of space, but were more of a nuisance than a danger. The fact that Oso was being such an asshole was just going to make it interesting for the gypsy from Valencia.

Pastor's first move was to keep in mind what Oso had told him about not telling anyone about their dealings together. He did everything but drive around in one of those old sound trucks with loudspeakers announcing to everyone he knew, and many he didn't, that he was going to be moving a serious amount of cocaine. It didn't take long before there was talk referring to Oso as the Pablo Escobar of gypsies, the Romani *El Chapo*.

Only two days later, this whirlwind of news reached Malaga and one of Oso's people who immediately passed it on to the boss, barely one week before the deal was to go down. The plan called for three kilograms of cocaine to change hands when Pastor drove down to the southern city, but Oso's people were hearing rumors of a load from three hundred to as much as a thousand kilos.

"You might have to change your nickname to Scarface, boss," one of Oso's gypsy homeboys said to him.

"That loudmouth little prick," Oso howled upon hearing the news.

The gossip about the shipment seemed to have struck with the force of a tsunami all over the Mediterranean coast.

When his phone rang with a call from Oso, Pastor was waiting and ready. After listening to two minutes of screaming, Pastor was finally able to get in a few words in his defense.

"*Primo*, "I didn't say a word about this to anyone," Pastor said. "My mother must have told everyone."

"Your mother? How did she know about it if you didn't tell her?"

"She must have looked at my phone. You sent a lot of messages about it," Pastor said.

"But I never said what we were doing. I was using code. How did she figure it out?"

In Oso's sophisticated word-substitution code "oranges" was used instead of "cocaine."

"She's clever. She probably told everyone because she's proud of me, says I'll be like you one day and have an American car and everything."

Pastor had never studied psychology, but he knew that peacocks lived for flattery. Once Oso was led to believe that he was some sort of role model, his demeanor changed immediately from rage to whatever vain people feel when their egos are stroked. Pastor decided to make a move before Oso's warm glow faded.

"Maybe we should back off on this for a while until this blow's over?"

"Naw, *primo*. Let's stick to the plan."

Although he'd spent his entire life in criminal activities, and two years in prison, Pastor never considered himself to be a gangster, and he'd never much admired the archetype. Although it was never spelled out, and certainly never written down, the gypsies had rules. It was complicated and so highly subjective to the point that everyone had their own interpretation, but the Romani did have a code, of a sort. It began with a hierarchy of relationships.

First of all, and of most importance, you had your immediate family. Next, the extended family, which for gypsies was almost a completely ridiculous exaggeration, something of a knot that would take a team of scientists specializing in DNA to untie. After this, was your clan which could be compared to what most *payos* call nationality.

Theft for a gypsy is a completely different concept than it is for most other people. Pickpocketing a wallet from a *payo* on a crowded bus, or stealing a bicycle chained to a streetlamp aren't considered acts of theft. Even though the wallet was in someone's back pocket, and the bike secured to a street post, for a gypsy, they are like things you'd find on the ground with no one else in sight. Why wouldn't you take them?

Most of the things proscribed by modern society were things that gypsies felt didn't apply to them, like they were outside of the jurisdiction. They felt they were the chosen people, chosen not to pay taxes, chosen not to work "real jobs" with bosses, chosen not to enter into life outside of their clans.

Pastor had nothing against dealing drugs. The prohibition against drugs meant nothing to him as a gypsy. If people wanted to do drugs, why would anyone else care? A gypsy would never argue against personal freedom, as their entire culture was based on this concept, for better or worse. Dealing drugs for a distant cousin was also something Pastor wouldn't find objectionable, but if you wanted to irritate him, all you needed to do was to give him orders. To say that taking orders wasn't one of his strong points would be an understatement along the lines that fire didn't play well with water.

It wasn't as if Pastor was afraid to tell his cousin that he'd taken himself out of the drug business, he just preferred to avoid the confrontation. He thought that announcing to the world that Oso had a huge drug deal in the works would scare him off, at least enough to keep Pastor out of any future operations, but Oso kept up the pressure.

"I need you down here in Malaga, you know, for the 'oranges' we talked about," he told Pastor on the phone only two days after their previous conversation.

Perhaps Oso was even dumber than Pastor had previously thought if he believed that simply substituting a few words would be enough to confound a police intercept. Pastor knew that it was highly unlikely that the cops were monitoring their calls, but even so, his cousin's stupidity was almost frightening.

If Oso wanted to be an idiot drug lord, Pastor decided that he needed to raise his own level of stupid. He showed up at Oso's meeting place in the outskirts of Malaga driving a dilapidated ice cream truck with a loudspeaker blaring the ditty "Pop Goes the Weasel" at a very uncomfortable decibel level. Before Pastor had even shut off the ignition, Oso and two of his men bounded out of the door of the abandoned warehouse with guns drawn.

"*Hola, primo*," Pastor said. "Check out my new undercover vehicle."

"What in the fuck is wrong with you?" Oso screamed at the top of his voice, lowering his pistol.

"I know, right? Who would suspect this truck to be carrying drugs?"

"Turn off that fucking loudspeaker," Oso screamed again.

Pastor made a vaudevillian farse of first turning up the volume of the recorded message to the decibel level of a 747 take-off, then blasting an ear-splitting screech of static feedback until finally there was silence.

"Pretty cool, huh? Cops will never suspect me."

"You fucking idiot," Oso couldn't stop screaming, as if his ears had been damaged by the auditory assault.

Among his many talents, Pastor was very convincing as an actor, an essential part of one of the most prized skills of the gypsies: lying. Pastor feigned injury at Oso's insult and disappointment that his idea with the ice cream truck wasn't appreciated.

"Don't you see?' Pastor asked as he waved his hand towards the truck. "It's undercover, *primo*. I customized the song, something I saw in an American movie. It's totally undercover, *primo*. I can even sell some ice cream so the cops won't suspect anything, just like *Miami Vice*."

The series was called something different in Spanish, *Corrupción en Miami*, and was a big hit among the gypsies who always cheered for the criminals on television and the movies. Just for emphasis, Pastor blasted the tune again throwing his cousin into an even deeper rage.

"Turn the shit off!" Oso screamed at the top of his lungs.

Pastor obliged and was led away by Oso, as if the proximity to the truck was toxis-

"You can't run dope in this ridiculous vehicle. What the hell is wrong with you?"

As he was admonishing his cousin, the loudspeaker in the truck began its recorded message once again at full volume which Pastor had turned on with a remote control in his pocket, counting on this full vaudeville comedy effect to push Oso over the edge completely. Oso was spitting in anger as he screamed at Pastor to drive the truck away and come back with a more appropriate vehicle for the cocaine transport.

"No problem, *primo*. I just need a couple of days."

Pastor found it almost impossible not to burst out laughing, but he held it in until he was driving away with the recording blaring once again. When he was still just outside of the warehouse, he was stopped to by three children waving handfuls of change to exchange for ice cream, which Pastor thoughtfully planned ahead of his meeting. He gave the kids the treats he'd brought along but didn't take their money, money he had given them earlier to play this part in his scene. He didn't look that way, but he knew Oso was watching, driving him further over the edge. When he showed up four days later, his entrance almost drove his cousin to violence.

"What in the fuck are you doing in a police car? Are you completely crazy?"

"What? It's the best way to transport drugs because who's going to stop a police car?"

Apoplectic with rage and incomprehension, Oso was on the verge of murder or cardiac arrest—he wasn't a healthy man.

"How in hell did you get a police car?"

"Everyone knows that cops always leave their keys in the ignition," Pastor said. "It was the easiest car I've ever stolen."

In fact, Pastor knew a guy who knew a guy who was friends with a local cop who felt that one hundred euros was a fair price to rent his patrol car for an hour.

Oso stood looking at Pastor sitting at the wheel of the patrol car.

"The idiot left it running on a bad street in Malaga. You can't leave a car unattended in a gypsy neighborhood. Everyone knows that, right? Must've been a rookie."

"Get that car the fuck out of here, now!" Oso screamed at the top of his lungs.

Pastor bowed his head in mock shame. He drove away, fishtailing and laying a patch of burned rubber in his wake with the lights on and the siren wailing.

Oso was having serious doubts about doing business with the gipsy from Valencia, cousin or no cousin.

"What's going to be this idiot's next big idea?" Oso asked his crew. "Maybe he'll decide to transport the drugs accompanied by a marching brass band."

Pastor hadn't thought of that, but he would have applauded the idea. Pastor found it absolutely astounding that his cousin was too stupid to realize that the very last thing Pastor wanted was to do any further business with him, but the fool called him again asking when he would show up again to make the deal.

"And just come in a regular fucking car. Stop trying to imitate something from TV."

The regular car Pastor arrived in the next afternoon rattled loudly after he turned off the ignition in front of Oso and two of his men. Pastor stepped out of the old Fiat and as he approached the group, the car hiccupped, restarted on its own, started belching sooty plumes of smoking diesel from under the hood, and burst into flames. Fortunately, one of Oso's men had an extinguisher in his van to end the farse quickly before the entire neighborhood was alerted to the disaster.

Oso had no choice but to pull the plug on this business relationship with his cousin. Pastor wondered if anyone had ever been obliged to work so hard and be so creative to get fired from a job.

Before Pastor could walk away from his ruined sedan and the promise of riches of a drug deal that wasn't to be, Oso offered other transactions they could do in the future. The fact that his cousin still wanted to work with him in spite of all of the effort Pastor had spent in painting himself as the most incompetent criminal in human history, obliged him to reconsider his estimation of Oso.

This shouldn't have surprised him. In prison, Pastor had known a man convicted of murdering his wife and child, yet he was a talented watercolorist and generous to a fault. Hell, someone told Pastor that even Hitler was nice to his dog.

Besides, he and Oso were cousins.

TRUNK REFLECTIONS

The old adage says we never regret things in life we did, only those we didn't. Couldn't disagree more as I squirmed in the trunk of a car, hands and feet bound securely with baling wire, deeply regretting something I did.

Did I deserve to be in this dire predicament? I thought it was a total over-reaction. After all, I'd broken no laws, just a commandment which aren't always crimes, right? Didn't even know she was married, and definitely not to mafia thug Pyotr Sokolov, the villain of this tale.

Pyotr looked like an underworld goon: a pillar of muscle, scar tissue, and Russian prison tattoos. Had I known he was the husband, I wouldn't have ventured into his hemisphere. No do-overs in this life, no mulligans, no turning back the clock, and no way to un-fuck his wife.

After flirting with her at the gym, she invited me to her place. No mention of a husband. Why would I ask? She was the hottest woman who'd ever so brazenly thrown herself at me—only an idiot would inquire about marital status. I'm a pig, not stupid. I wanted to ask Pyotr what he would've done, but when he kidnapped me in the gym parking lot the next day, he was in no mood for talking, beating me unconscious without saying a word. So much for two sides to every story.

To add insult to his injury, after my tryst with Mrs. Goon, I allegedly left the door ajar allowing his cat to bolt, a pet he'd cherished for eleven years. He was more inconsolable over the missing cat than the infidelity. Unfair blaming me about the cat, but as far as debauching the Tenth Commandment, guilty as charged, your honor. Don't remember all of them, but we probably violated other Commandments just during foreplay.

I came to in the trunk, the traffic noise gradually fading until I heard gravel slapping the undercarriage. After a sharp left, the car slowed and started pitching and rolling, indicating a dirt road. After stopping, Pyotr opened the trunk just long enough to grab a shovel before furiously slamming it shut again, still not saying a word.

I heard the sound of shoveling. The pace was furious, like someone in a grave digging race.

"Dude, what's the hurry? You're gonna pull a muscle," I screamed. "Let's talk this over."

It was obvious I'd be dead soon, just wondered if the end would be preceded by another torture session from the cat-loving psychopath.

Then I heard scratching in the corner of the trunk. An animal? Was this the torture? An enraged badger to rip me to shreds? I couldn't see anything in the complete darkness but felt something licking my face.

And purring.

The trunk opened and the cat leapt into the gangster's arms.

"Snowball!" Pyotr squealed.

I bent around to look at them and felt a crowbar beneath me.

Take every maudlin airport reunion you've witnessed along with every tearful Hallmark movie homecoming, together they didn't compare to Pyotr's sobbing relief on finding that damn cat. It's strange to be embarrassed for a guy who tortured, hog-tied you, and just finished digging your grave, but I wanted to tell Pyotr to get a room already.

Could he be so happy he'd let bygones be bygones? Thank fuck he couldn't see the play-by-play on my phone videos; I didn't give up my password even after he slammed my hand in the door. Once again, I can't regret things I didn't do with his spouse because we did everything, possibly inventing a few positions destined to become urban legends after being anointed with comedically vulgar names.

"Forgiveness" wasn't in the Russian's limited vocabulary as he savagely pulled my hair trying to drag me out of the trunk.

"I didn't screw your wife," I screamed in a last-ditch survival effort. "I'm gay."

He smiled, dropping his pants.

"Prove it."

"Can't do it tied up, honey." I chirped.

He untwisted the wire from my wrists. When the feeling returned, I gripped the crowbar with both hands.

Pyotr was about to regret everything he did, at least to me. He'd already dug his own grave.

I'll worry about his orphaned cat later.

TOUGH GUYS

Life in organized crime on the streets of New York wasn't what it used to be, just ask anyone over the age of sixty, anyone who'd been in the life. The FBI had all but wiped out the mafia family hierarchies, and most of the Italian organizations couldn't compete with the Hispanic drug cartels, not in New York and not anywhere outside of Italy. The African-American gangs had the numbers, and their rank and file made the old-school Italians look like risk-adverse Boy Scouts when it came to conflict resolution. Like with the Mexicans, they valued ruthlessness over everything else, and any thought of jail time wasn't in their planning equations.

Even with its glory years far behind, the mob life still had its appeal for guys like Richie and Trey, twenty-somethings who bragged that they never had a job that required a social security number. They had little to show for their life of crime now and wouldn't have a dime coming to them if they ever made it to retirement age—a rather farfetched idea to both of the young hoods, and anyone who knew them.

They'd grown up on the same street in Brooklyn, watched the same gangster movies, dropped out of school together at sixteen, and entered the criminal justice system as juveniles six months later. In juvie, they'd learned the importance of being a part of a group, it was the only way to stay safe, the only way to survive. They both considered themselves to be survivors, and if no one else had their backs, they took care of each other.

As brutal as juvenile detention was in the state of New York, it really hadn't prepared either of them for the adult system. Trey was the first to find himself at Ryker's Island while he awaited his court date for an assault charge with his best friend getting locked up four months later. Ryker's Island was whole new education for the two white boys from Brooklyn who tried to act tough but were scared shitless every minute inside.

However, the two had just enough in the way of connections from the city to remain above water, barely, just by their nostrils, but it was better than the total hell the unconnected slobs endured. Shakedowns, beatings, humiliation, and murder were more common than an outsider could ever imagine. Welcome to the American criminal justice system, where violence where fellow inmates cause each other more misery than the guards, bars, and walls put together.

Richie had been out after serving thirteen months; Trey was released just before Christmas six months later. After their releases, it had taken both of them less than twenty-four hours to commit their first, post-prison felonies. For the purposes of their parole, both were living together with Richie's grandmother in a two-bedroom walk-up in Bay Ridge, but they had plans to move out after an old acquaintance from their neighborhood set them up with a burglary job that was going to be their biggest score ever.

The home was supposed to be empty in the evening, but the idiot walked in on them as they were heisting an impressive amount of high-tech gear. Trey didn't hesitate, not for a second. He unleashed a barrage of kicks and punches that left the guy unconscious and bleeding profusely. He must have been at least sixty years old. They took their time after that and cleaned the place out of everything small and of value, including a silver flatware set. Richie wanted to give the set to his grandmother, but Trey made him come to his senses.

They sold the entire lot to their contact. It was enough to score the apartment and have a few nights of high living on the town.

"My man," Richie said as he raised his glass in the Manhattan nightclub. "You were fearless. Didn't bat an eye, didn't even give it a thought, and just lit into him."

"Nothing to think about. We had work to do," Trey said clinking his glass with Richie's and taking a drink of the expensive vodka, not particularly good vodka, but everything was expensive in Manhattan—too expensive for two half-assed gangsters.

Trey knew that if he had any trouble with the sixty-year-old in the apartment, Richie would have been there to back him up. Just like in this over-priced, very lower-tier Manhattan nightclub. Any asshole gives them shit; they'd take him apart. That's one thing the organized crime life still had to offer: protection and at least some degree of unity. You put your hands on someone from the organization; you have to deal with all of them. This almost always meant they rarely had to actually fight anyone, and never one-on-one. Richie and Trey did everything they could to look tough, starting with their garish prison tattoos and military boots even if they were wearing suits like they were on this across-the-bridge outing.

This supposed mobster moral code usually amounted to little more than a group of thugs ganging up to stomp anyone who so much as looked at any of them the wrong way. Of course, none of the assholes in this place knew who they were, but back in their corner of Brooklyn, people would steer clear of them, or else. The people here didn't seem to notice them at all, like they were invisible. Here, they were just two nobodies trying to celebrate their score in a roomful of what they figured were Wall Street types and fashion model wannabes who never gave them as much as a glance. They should have stayed in Bay Ridge where they at least knew some people, although even there it seemed there were fewer and fewer of the old crowd around these days. No one could afford it.

They decided to go back home, taking a taxi even though they couldn't afford it. The train just seemed like slumming since they were wearing new suits.

Their once rough neighborhood was quickly changing into renovated townhomes and new low-rise condominiums, with franchise boutiques and wine bars, where even the corner dive bars were being turned into hangouts for the new bourgeoise class.

"None of these faggots would last thirty seconds in prison," Trey said as he scanned the clientele of their favorite corner bar, now hip-deep in hipsters and women couples with short hair and tattoos playing old rock classics on the ancient jukebox.

"Whatever, we'll be robbing all of these idiots like that pussy from last night." Richie said with a slight lack of conviction that even he noted.

They both felt out of place in this bar that they'd known since way before they were legally allowed to drink there, not that they mentioned this to each other, and they fought desperately not to think it themselves. It was too much like admitting they'd already lost in life, and they weren't even 30. They didn't see much in the way of a career path in their line of work. Not that they'd use words like "career path" but they weren't so stupid not to see the writing on the wall. They couldn't name one example of anyone they knew who'd become even remotely successful as a hoodlum.

A bearded guy walked up to the bar and stepped between the two, muttering an "excuse me" and ordering a pitcher of beer for his table. He bumped Trey's arm slightly, not even enough for him to spill a drop of his beer.

"What the fuck, dude? Get the fuck away from me before I wreck you," Trey shouted over The Who song blaring through the new sound system.

"What?" the clueless hipster asked.

Trey grabbed the hipster by his beard and pulled their faces together.

"I said, get the fuck away from me."

The hipster walked back to his table without taking the pitcher the bartender had already set down on the bar.

Richie bumped fists with his friend and they both had a hearty laugh at the hipster's expense who was probably an actual homeowner in the neighborhood, while neither of the two tough guys had yet to pay taxes in their not-so-short adult lives. Yet they felt the newbies didn't belong here.

By some miracle that defied the usual odds, both of them left the bar before closing and mostly sober—not that the night was over. The hyper-expensive drinks in Manhattan slowed their buzz as had the long taxi ride back to Bay Ridge. They were far from finished for the evening, but their corner bar was almost as alien as the nightclub across the bridge. They were on to their next choice they hoped hadn't been overrun by the new Brooklyn elite.

Douchebags and pussies, all.

They walked down the street side-by-side, intimidating anyone in their path and pushing people out of the way.

A young, good-looking couple walked hand-in-hand towards them. Trey refused to let them pass and almost knocked the guy down.

"Hey, what the hell, man?" the girl shouted.

"Shut up, cunt," Trey shouted back.

The young couple froze, the guy telling his partner to keep quiet before they walked on.

Trey had a big laugh and slapped Richie on the back.

"I could not fucking live with myself if I were such a pussy, I swear," Trey said.

"Dude, I hear you."

They only had a few blocks to reach their next destination, but they felt flush with money and decided to cab it. Trey stepped off the curb and threw his right hand in the air while giving an ear-piercing whistle—a valuable talent to have in New York. A taxi approached, but another guy was also flagging it a few meters down the street. The taxi started to pull to a stop and the guy turned around to take the hand of a woman he was escorting, Trey strode towards the couple and shouted at the guy.

"This is my cab, asshole."

The guy let go of the woman's hand and turned towards Trey who was soon joined by Richie.

"Your cab? Dude, do you live in New York? I'm farther down the block. It's mine. These are simple rules."

"Fuck off, cunt. It's ours."

Trey was shouting.

The guy motioned for the girl to step away and back up to the curb.

"Are you for real? You're losing your mind over a taxi? A taxi that I hailed a half a block ahead of you two?" the guy asked in a calm voice.

"I said, fuck off, cunt. Get the fuck out of here."

The guy gave Trey a look, then started to turn away towards the curb and the very worried girl waiting for him.

"It's all yours, tough guy," he said.

This made Trey even more furious. He grabbed the guy roughly by his shoulder as he walked away.

Without the slightest hesitation, the guy who was shorter than Trey by a head, turned and landed a blow to Trey's temple. The bigger man dropped like a stone, unconscious and pissing himself immediately.

Richie stepped forward and threw a haymaker that only grazed the top of the guy's head. The guy reached up and grabbed Richie's throat with his thumb and index finger and clamped down like a vice. Richie dropped to his knees. The guy kicked Richie in the solar plexus with the toe of his shoe. Richie thought he was going to die right then and there. He fell face-down in the street gasping for air.

The guy walked the girl delicately around the two incapacitated morons lying in the street, Trey still unconscious and Richie writhing in agony. The smart couple stepped into the taxi and drove off.

According to their hallowed mafia code of honor, the guy who fucked them up had signed his own death warrant, but Trey and Richie never mentioned the incident to anyone, they didn't even talk about to each other, and the last fucking thing either of them really wanted was to run into that guy again, not that they could have picked him out of a line-up of only two people.

Two days later, Richie went back to the corner bar to apply for a job as a line cook. He'd written his social security number on his wrist. Someone told him they'd probably ask for it.

TO DO LIST

Distracted by household errands wasn't the best mindset while pulling down a score. Why didn't the wife make a list? Expected him to move heaven and earth today just because she had one extra shift this week. It's not like all he did was sit in front of the TV watching fishing shows. He worked five nights at the tavern, and now he was here, which was like two shifts in one day, right? But when you got three kids, you have to multi-task like a street juggler on a unicycle.

Too bad he only had this car for the job—much nicer than his normal piece of crap. Couldn't afford anything else with his insurance, not after two DUIs. Walking everywhere was out of the question when you had kids. Besides, tough guys don't walk. They also shouldn't drive ten-year-old Toyotas.

This ride still smelled new, at least before he'd chain-smoked a half dozen Marlboros. Normally, he tossed the butts out the window, but he didn't want some do-gooder giving him grief for littering, bothering him while he waited, trying to think of everything he needed to do as soon they finished up inside and he got them the hell out of here.

Pick up stuff for the sink. If his old lady bitched about that drip one more time, he'd lose it. It's not like he was too lazy to replace a washer; just wasn't sure he could. He'd done it before, but the kitchen faucet looked complicated. He procrastinated only because he feared failure. He learned that in group during his last stretch doing time. He was afraid that if he couldn't figure it out, he'd have to call a plumber.

Plumbers, now those were the real criminals. Fifty bucks minimum just to walk in the door. He shelled out a week's salary at the tavern just to repair the shower last year. The crook charged four hours, taking his sweet time about it. A nice score for a morning's work with no gun and no risk of landing in prison.

He needed stuff from the supermarket. As he sat and smoked, he tried desperately to remember everything: cleaning products, and a few things for pasta *putanesca* they didn't have at the house. What went into that? He taught her how to make it, and now he was drawing a total blank. He had a few other things on his mind as he idled in front of the bank in a tow-away zone.

He was praying that he could buy new school backpacks for the kids at the supermarket, killing two birds and all that. Of course, they wouldn't settle for just any bookbag. Nope, they needed exactly what every other brat their age slung over one shoulder. Not giving in to their demands was like some new form of child abuse, at least that's probably how his prick parole officer would see it. What did they want?

Ironman, Frozen, and Sponge Bob.

Yes!

He breathed a sigh of relief after pulling those three tidbits of trivia out of his butt. He was doing his best to make up for lost time with the kids. He wrote down these important yet ephemeral markers in their lives. No way he'd remember later.

He was thinking about what he carried his books in when he heard a gunshot.

He turned towards the door just as his two accomplices backed out, firing another round into the ceiling. He had a .45 under his right leg, but he didn't need it; they were just making a statement. The masked pair jumped in the back. He floored it with the bank alarm fading as they sped away. He looked down at the digital clock on the dash: 12:57. A lot to do and his shift at the tavern started at six. Being a little late on a Tuesday wasn't a crime.

Italian pasta sauces were simple. Five ingredients, tops.

He bashed the steering wheel furiously with both fists while slamming on the brakes.

Capers! He needed capers.

"The hell you doing?" the two heavily-armed men screamed from the back seat.

"Have to write something down. It's kinda important."

THANKS FOR THE MEMORIES

Arthur Andrews sat on a divan near the mirrors as his father tried on a new suit at the upscale downtown department store. Arthur was nine years old, looked even younger, but talked like a seasoned Mafia enforcer. As he spoke to his father, he balanced the conversation by hurling threats and other vitriol into his cell phone headset.

"I already got me a suit, Arthur. The one I wear Sundays," Mr. Andrews said.

The father's discomfort was audible.

"This is a business suit, dad. How many times do I have to tell you? You need it for your new job," Arthur says to his father while into the cell phone he screams, "Cut him off. Do I have to do everything? He's already down three Gs."

"I don't apprehend what's wrong with my old job. I liked it. I was good at it."

"We've been over this before, dad. Don't be so resistant to advancement and self-improvement."

"The other guys down at the shop see me wearing this to work, well, let me tell you, I'll never hear the end of it."

"Just get over the fact that you are leaving those proletarian slobs behind, dad. You're moving into management."

"I just wish I could go back to wearing my canvas work pants and boots like I been doing all this time. I don't need to wear no suit, even in management, not at Al's Appliance Superstore."

Mr. Andrews had worked in the service department of Al's Appliance for the past twelve years until Arthur decided that he wanted his father to move into the realm of white-collar employment.

"It's all about image, dad. You have to look like a leader."

Arthur returned to giving a hostile earful to whoever had the unenviable task of being on the other end of the conversation. Arthur Andrews was extremely interested in image these days, ever since he read about those punks in the British royal family in a gossip rag.

"Look at what this thing costs. I paid less for my first car. You and me could go see the races every day for a year for the same money."

"And no more NASCAR, dad. I want you to play golf—it's more dignified."

The once-unctuous salesman was becoming less so with every country-accented word, malapropism, solecism, and grammar gaff that Arthur's father uttered.

"Perhaps you'd be more comfortable shopping in our discount store, sir. Of course, they don't carry these brands…"

The salesman turned to address Arthur as it was painfully obvious that the son was in charge of this outing. Papa bear was only along for the ride.

Arthur cut off the clerk with a raised finger as he yelled into his phone.

"You, Slasher, Frankie One Eye, Ice Pick, Rat Face, and Peanut pick him up and throw him out. And don't be gentle about it! Got it?"

Arthur gave his cell phone a moment of respite and returned his attention to the salesman.

"Listen," he began while shaking his head dismissively, pitifully, "I'm sure what you make, along with your store discount, go further over there at Bargain World, or whatever vulgar name you call it, but my dad can't be seen in the kind of off-brand stuff you wear."

Before the salesman had time to recover, Arthur was standing on a stool and straightening his father's new tie.

"Shoot the cuffs, dad."

Mr. Andrews obeyed and looked at himself approvingly in the mirror.

"He'll take this one and the one in charcoal. Put it on this card."

Arthur dismissed the defeated clerk with the wave of a credit card. If Arthur's father wondered how his son was going to pay for his very impressive new wardrobe, he was too afraid to ask him about it. Arthur was a little touchy lately, it was better just to let him have his way.

The Andrews had always been intimidated by their only child. Arthur had scored off the charts on every intelligence test that the public schools had thrown at him. Even as a baby he was peculiar. His mother would try to make him watch the Walt Disney cartoons like the other kids in the neighborhood. Little Arthur would howl like a banshee until she took out "The Little Mermaid" and put in one of her husband's movies, preferably a gangster classic.

When he was two, little Arthur's favorite movie was "Reservoir Dogs." His parents were both proud and mortified that he could recite every line of dialogue by heart. The Andrews's only heir especially loved to act out the scene where the cop gets his ear sliced off. After that, they could put the little guy down for the night and he wouldn't move until morning.

They were extremely proud of their son, although sometimes his high IQ was a burden to them, like how Arthur corrected his mother's grammar so often that she quit talking altogether when he was about five.

"Daddy and me are going to put you in the college preparatory first grade class."

"It's 'Daddy and *I* are going to put you in the college preparatory first grade class.' Don't bother, I'm sure I'll be bored to death."

Arthur's mother wasn't as thick-skinned as her inarticulate husband, and soon resorted to communicating with her only child by whistling and gestures to avoid grammatical imperfection. She and her son quickly developed their own language completely free of the rules of grammar that had once so hindered their conversation, at least as far as Arthur was concerned.

The Andrews refused to let Arthur skip ahead several grades as school administrators had suggested. They wanted their son to have a normal life, as if that would be possible with Arthur's freakishly high intelligence. Arthur quickly learned that he could do whatever he wanted in school, or not do whatever he chose not to do.

Any sort of discipline became impossible once Arthur determined that he could hold the school ransom by refusing to take any standardized tests if they tried to punish him for any of his misdeeds. He single-handedly raised the school's test scores enough to keep them comfortably above minimum requirements. If Arthur were to fail a test purposefully, it could mean that the entire district might have to sacrifice federal aid money. He had them by the short hairs. They knew it, and he most definitely knew it.

Arthur seemed content to live out his childhood in a sort of "don't ask, don't tell" détente between himself and the usual sources of authority for normal kids. With his exceptional intelligence and extremely ordinary homelife, Arthur seemed completely uninterested in the world outside of his own thoughts and imagination.

Until one day when Arthur picked up that fateful copy of *People* magazine in the office of his father's realtor. Mr. Andrews had brought Arthur along with him so that his son could explain to the realtor the complicated refinancing scheme he'd worked out for his parents. Normally Arthur wouldn't be caught dead reading celebrity gossip trash, but *People* was all that was available. The magazine had a feature story with several photographs chronicling the life of the British royal family. There were pictures of young princes riding horseback, visiting chic European vacation destinations, and other activities of the leisure class. Arthur immediately compared their lives with his and saw that his own childhood was coming up short.

In fourth grade, Arthur had begun an extensive study of childhood development. He read all of the research on the traumatic effects of neglect in preadolescent children. Now Arthur was concerned that his lack of experience with summers spent on the French Riviera and black-tie balls in the company of important and influential adults might one day come back to haunt him. It's not that he thought that his own childhood could be described as unhappy in any way, but felt he should cover his bases by having experiences like the rich creeps in the magazine. To have what they had, he'd need more money, a lot more.

Once Arthur had decided to focus his mental gifts on making money, it didn't take him long to soar, and his love of gangster films directed him to a life of crime as the quickest path to instant wealth. He started a casino and employed his group of unsavory friends to staff it—if "unsavory" is an appropriate term to use when describing fifth graders.

Whether they were Arthur's classmates or not, some of them gave Mrs. Andrews the creeps. She wasn't concerned that they'd have a bad influence on Arthur. Arthur had been above any influence from his peers, and it was pretty obvious he was the ringleader of his little group; it was Arthur who had given all of them those dreadful nicknames. She just wished that Arthur could have cute little friends that she could fuss over. Lord knows she could never fuss over Arthur himself; he was the least needy child on the planet. Arthur rarely even took meals at home these days. He was spending more of his time at that Boy's Club.

The Boy's Club was a front for Arthur's gambling operation. He had rented a warehouse a few blocks from his house for what would soon become the most successful criminal venture in the city's history. Arthur kept it simple; he wasn't about to overestimate the abilities of his staff. He had three blackjack tables, a roulette wheel, a craps table, but his biggest earner was the sports book.

As gifted as Arthur was in academics, his true genius was in picking winners in professional football. He'd beaten the Las Vegas bookies on four out of the last five regular season NFL games. He picked all of the winners and covered the spread in the first two rounds of the playoffs. His odds for the two division championship games were in stark contrast to the Las Vegas numbers. If his luck lasted this week, he'd be a very wealthy fifth grader.

It would be difficult to believe it from his appearance, but Arthur wasn't really interested in the money. Ever since he saw that issue of *People,* he'd become obsessed with acquiring his own collection of happy childhood memories. When he noticed that all the rich kids' parents drove big off-road vehicles, he leased the biggest one he could find for his mother. She couldn't drive it very well and was completely terrified of the thing, but Arthur was more comfortable with the image it portrayed. It was a miracle that his mother hadn't killed anyone so far. She'd often get home and find a tricycle stuck in the wheel well or streaks of paint on the bumpers, but never any blood.

Arthur was never interested in playing sports, but he felt that they were probably part of a happy childhood. He joined a youth soccer league although he rarely played—most of the time he sat on the sidelines furiously pecking on his laptop or shouting instructions into his cell phone. Although if you pressed him, Arthur couldn't tell you which team he played for, but he almost always made the winning goal, week after week.

The same scenario suspiciously unfolded at each game. The score would be tied with less than a minute to go. Arthur would put down his laptop and phone to come off the sideline from the bench. He'd get the pass and dribble in front of the goal. Just as the goalie tripped over his own feet, Arthur would kick the ball in for the winning goal. Sometimes he'd miss and they'd have to repeat the pantomime. You can't put a price tag on childhood memories like those, but if, just for the sake of argument, you were looking for a price, it would be somewhere around $50 for every player, coach, and referee. This doesn't include the photographer's salary. Priceless memories need good pictures.

Arthur insisted that his mother drive him to soccer. He could just as easily take a taxi like he did for school every day (the bus, or "loser cruiser" as he called it, was too noisy, slow, and full of cretins) but kids' mothers were supposed to drive them to soccer practice. When Arthur's father offered to drive him one day, Arthur screamed at him that there were no such things as soccer dads. Dads are too busy to drive their kids to soccer. His teammates would think that Mr. Andrews had nothing better to do, not that he did.

Arthur's mom continued to chauffeur him even though she wasn't getting the hang of driving the monster truck he'd forced on her. She would've had an easier time skippering an aircraft carrier on the high seas.

Arthur's plans for his perfect childhood were moving along nicely. He picked both winners in the division playoff games and the other operations at the casino were all highly profitable. Things were going so well that he gave his boys a day off and invited them over to his house. As much of a tyrant as he was in business, Arthur also understood the value of positive motivation. All they needed was for the entertainment to arrive.

"Hey Arthur, you have two women here to see you," his father said through the locked bedroom door.

"Some of the guys are falling behind so I got them these math tutors."

Arthur left the explanation at that as he led the two scantily-clad young women back to the party in his bedroom. Mr. Andrews was about to comment that they didn't have any books with them before he thought better of it and returned to his TV show. Like so many other things dealing with Arthur's personal life, Mr. Andrews knew it didn't pay to jump to conclusions. After a couple of hours of hooting and hollering from Andrew's bedroom, the two "tutors" let themselves out the front door while counting fistfuls of bills. Mr. Andrews thought that lots of tutors probably get paid in small bills and dress like round card girls at a prize fight.

Mr. Andrews noticed that his son was becoming increasingly irritated. Arthur was on edge, no doubt about it. The other day at breakfast Mr. Andrews was commenting on an article in the paper about a kid being tried as an adult when Arthur when into a half-hour tirade on America's immoral judicial system that unfairly targets youthful offenders. Mr. Andrews noticed that his son was fairly obsessed with the issue. While other kids were doing oral reports on whether or not chocolate milk should be served in the cafeteria, Arthur was lecturing anyone who would listen on recent Supreme Court rulings against minors.

Not that Arthur's growing empire had much of a risk of having problems with the law; the rank-and-file members of the local police force were mostly degenerate gamblers and some of his best customers. Arthur's picks thus far in the play-offs had devastated the police gamblers, and most of the cops were so far in debt to him that he was considering a direct deposit system. The lawyer for the police union had pitched this idea to Arthur as a way to help pay off his debt to the casino.

He'd convinced everyone in town that his untaxed casino was not only a victimless crime, but a public service. Arthur had achieved a status for gambling that was the envy of organized crime. Arthur should have realized from the Mafia films that he so admired that gangsters have their own way of dealing with envy.

Five days before the Super Bowl, Arthur came home from a long and profitable shift at the casino and found his parents duct taped to dining room chairs and four thugs on the sofa watching *Funniest Home Videos*.

"You can take the tape off her mouth, she doesn't talk much these days," Arthur said as he reached for the remote and turned to *Firing Line*.

"Hey Harry Potter Capone, shut your face," said a fat guy in a bowling shirt.

They all got a laugh out of that.

"My employer, Mr. Digotti, is shutting you down. We're gonna take over all of your action for the game. If you want to make a bet, you can do it with Mr. Digotti and I."

"You mean 'Mr. Digotti and me.'"

"Wha?"

"Never mind."

If Arthur was the least bit concerned, he was hiding it well as he made himself a ham sandwich and sat down in front of the TV.

"Guys, can this wait? I really want to watch this program."

The head thug in the bowling shirt seemed a little confused with Arthur's entirely reasonable request; he was more accustomed to a man begging for his life.

"Turn it off," he grunted.

"Listen, I know that you aren't going to harm a nine-year-old kid, so what other choice do you have but to let me watch my show? When it's over I promise I'll listen to whatever dire threats you were sent here to deliver."

Arthur turned the volume up and set down the remote control.

The TV show ended. The Mafia guys sat thoughtfully on the couch. Arthur's parents were still duct taped to the chairs, but their mouths were no longer covered, and the chairs had been moved allowing them to see the television. Arthur hit the mute button on the remote.

"Who woulda thought the Federal Reserve chairman had so much power?" Bowling shirt thug asked. "I mean, you raise the prime rate a half a percent and the whole economy starts tankin'."

"I didn't realize that Greenspan cost old man Bush the election in'92," one of the lower echelon thugs added. "What a dick."

Lower echelon thug turned to Mrs. Andrews.

"Pardon me, ma'am."

"Can we get to the matter at hand, gentlemen? I have a lot of work to do."

Arthur said as he pulled out his laptop and began pecking at the keyboard.

"If I understand you correctly you want me to stop taking action on the game. Let me just talk this over with my associates."

Just then Arthur's crew of little league henchman walked in without knocking. For fifth graders, they carried a fairly threatening presence.

"Good evening Mr. and Mrs. Andrews," they said in chorus.

Even in a show of force, the little hoodlums knew enough to show proper respect for the boss's parents.

"What're these little punks gonna do, not deliver my newspaper in the morning?"

Bowling shirt guy had quite the sense of humor.

The half-pint they called Ice Pick pulled a big squirt gun out of his backpack. This cracked up the four normal-size thugs in attendance.

"You'll laugh and then you'll cry. There's a half gallon of habanero pepper spray in this thing of my own creation. One drop of this stuff is enough to reduce a seven-foot grizzly to a blubbering bearskin rug."

"Hey boss, I seen that on the Nature Channel. I'd rather take a slug right in the gut," the lower echelon thug said as they all made their way wearily to the door.

"I didn't get your names, but just so there aren't any hard feelings, let me comp you guys some chips at my casino. Come by and introduce yourselves,"

Arthur said as he handed each thug a generous stack and escorted them   out. Arthur wasn't naïve enough to think that was going to be the end of it. He knew the tiresome mob honor dictated there must be several rounds of retribution and counter-retribution. That was the life they'd all chosen, except that Arthur despised people who talked in clichés, even if heavily-armed men surrounded them. The members of Arthur's crew were quite a bit more sociopathic than their leader and they were begging him to escalate this into a full-scale war. Arthur didn't object to violence as a management tool, but he was thinking of the long-term consequences. Fifth-grade Arthur thought that middle-age Arthur might be traumatized by the fact that a gang war had broken out in the middle of his childhood. He thought he could out-muscle this Mr. Digotti grease ball, but he was positively certain

79

that he could out-smart him. No, Arthur thought that a nonviolent approach was best—not the Gandhi, turn-the-other-cheek brand of nonviolence, but a malicious variety of nonviolence.

The key would be to hurt the Mafia guys in their earning capacity. Arthur had already done a fairly respectable job of scoping out this Mr. Digotti, but where he'd once seen him only as a competitor, they were now enemies. One of Digotti's main operations, and his de facto clubhouse, was a strip club on the north end of town.

"Peanut, give me everything you got on the Deja-Vu strip club," Arthur said to his shortest minion. "Slasher, you and Rat Face go mobile and head up there to 1009 North Blanchard. I'll text you with further instructions."

Peanut printed a seven-page file on the Deja-Vu and handed it to his boss. Arthur looked over the file and immediately found what he needed. From a desk drawer he took out a small electronic device and gave it to Peanut.

"Use this voice box and call all the dancers at the club and tell them their shift is canceled tonight. There's a female empowerment and self-esteem workshop they are required to attend at the Holiday Inn."

The voice box was one of Arthur's inventions that could change the sound of a human voice to any human voice that you sampled. All they had to do was record a few sentences of one of the club managers and they could duplicate his voice. Peanut called the dancers posing as the manager and told them to take the week off with pay and a bonus. He also instructed them that under no circumstances were they to call the club or to answer any phone calls from anyone associated with the club. There were Top Secret dealings going on and they weren't part of it. Next, Arthur instructed Slasher and Rat Face to change the marquee on the club from "Live Nude Girls" to "Amish Night, Every Night!"

The plan was to destroy the night's business at the club. Arthur wasn't surprised at just how much damage he did on the first night of his campaign of terror, but he was more than a little surprised to discover that there were actually two Amish fetishists in the town.

They were the only customers at the Deja-vu and were promptly ejected after hounding the staff about when the Amish act was coming on. After they left in their horse and buggy, the parking lot was completely empty. Arthur had taken this round.

Of course, there would be some sort of retaliatory gesture, or gestures. That's the way it was in all of the mob movies Arthur had memorized. Arthur expected something fairly serious, but even he was a bit surprised by Mr. Digotti's heavy-handed response to the strip club gag. Police investigators found over three hundred shell casings at the scene of what was to be called "the recess massacre" at Arthur's grade school.

It was meant as just a warning, but Ice Pick took a slug in the leg and Peanut was slightly injured when he dove under the merry-go-round. Arthur wasn't even at school that day—not that he'd ever condescend to participate in recess. He said that recess was for wimps. Arthur had called in sick so that he could cover as much Super Bowl action on this last weekday before the game. On the strength of his outstanding picks in the last half of the season and thus far in the playoffs, he was actually tilting the Las Vegas odds gradually away from Pittsburgh and towards the Seattle Seahawks.

Arthur heard about the shooting almost immediately. Ice Pick was recovering from surgery for the bullet wound, and Peanut was being held for observation for injuries suffered while under the merry-go-round. Arthur wondered if this incident would somehow traumatize him later in life even though he wasn't there. Arthur decided that enough was enough. He dialed Mr. Digotti's cell phone.

"Hello," answered the mafia don.

"Dude, that was just completely rude," Arthur said.

"That is but a trifling of what I will do to you and your associates if you fail to heed the warnings that I have instructed others to impose upon you to carry out without question and to the letter."

"What the hell are you trying to say? Stop talking like that. You sound like the world's worst fortune cookie writer," Arthur shouted.

"Shut down your gambling operations or you'll end up in a dumpster, kid."

"That's better. At least I understand you now. But here's the truth: I need this last game. After that I'm out. I promise."

Arthur had actually processed several thousand dollars in wagers online since he'd begun this conversation. He had three other phones on his desk that had been ringing constantly.

"Listen, I'd love to talk but I'm really busy right now."

"I'm not gonna warn you again, kid," Digotti screamed.

"Losing your temper is never good in business. Just keep this thought in your little head, tough guy. There are some fates worse than death. That is my threat to you, so back off or you'll understand what I'm saying. I have to get back to the calls. Go Seahawks!"

Arthur hung up and manned the other phones, two at a time.

***

The next wave of retribution from the Digotti camp occurred on Saturday morning in a group of coordinated attacks against Arthur's operations. Arthur was impressed by the extent of the assaults if not by their originality. Several of his employees had their BMX bikes vandalized, every window of the casino was smashed, and there were several incidents of personal attacks. Three of Arthur's boys received severe wedgies, and someone put gum in Frankie One Eye's hair. For safety reasons, Arthur had sent his parents out of town for the weekend, and he moved his operations to a suite at a downtown hotel. Digotti didn't have too many moves available to him at this point.

Arthur had nothing but options and he planned to use all of them.

Digotti was planning a huge Super Bowl party at the Deja-vu. They installed three new big-screen TVs on the dance floor. They anticipated a $50,000 day on strictly legitimate business on top of all of the wagering that would be going on right up until the end of the game. The final game of the season was a big tradition at the Deja-vu. Mr. Digotti himself manned the barbecue grills in the back lot. It was Mr. Digotti's pride and joy, his annual gala.

The Super Bowl was a day of truce, a sort of cease fire between rival gangs in the city. Arthur knew that every no-neck thug and nickel-and-dime gangster would be at the strip club for the Super Bowl party. It was their one day of unity as they all cheered for the same team—the spread.

Even with every tough guy within fifty miles in attendance, Arthur saw the party as a turtle on its back with its soft spot exposed to the world. Striking out at Digotti's football bash would be more than retribution and revenge for Arthur, it was going to be entertainment, it would be performance art, and it was going to be too easy to pass up.

Ice Pick checked himself out of the hospital that same day because his room didn't have cable TV. Peanut's injuries were more severe than a gunshot wound, something not at all difficult to understand if you've ever looked under a merry-go-round or under any other piece of playground equipment. He had to undergo boosters for typhoid and tetanus with cholera treatment thrown in just to be on the safe side. He was released early Saturday morning and met up with the rest of the gang in Arthur's bedroom to get their assignments for what was soon to be called Operation Overkill.

Arthur knew that the smart move would have been to simply take his winnings thus far and whatever he would make on the game and walk away so that he could concentrate solely on building his perfect childhood memories. That is what he started this whole business for in the first place. He had gone toe-to-toe with the local Mafia boss and got away with it with only the scratches picked up by Ice Pick and Peanut. Firing off a couple dozen Uzi clips into a schoolyard was fairly reprehensible behavior, but what really pushed Arthur to carry out the final blow against Digotti was the sheer arrogance and stupidity of the man.

In the midst of all of his plans for the Super Bowl and Operation Overkill, Arthur had a bit of overdue business of his own to look after. He had a childhood to live out. He knew that all too soon he would be an adult and he would need happy memories to look back upon to get him through the tough times. At least this is what he had read in all of the self-help books on the best seller list and in countless textbooks on childhood development.

On a personal level, he thought that childhood was pretty overrated. Arthur had never played with toys, and the games that most kids enjoyed bored him half-to-death. Take hide-and-seek, for instance. What was the point? The only thing Arthur liked about it was when he was "it" he could send his friends off to hide and then sit down and read a book undisturbed for thirty minutes. His playmates would straggle back one-by-one to find Arthur sitting in a lawn chair reading a chemistry text.

"You guys really did a great job of hiding. I couldn't find anyone."

No matter how many times Arthur pulled that one on them, they were always proud of themselves.

Just beneath the surface Arthur knew that he really wasn't missing anything, but he wanted to cover his bases on this whole happy childhood concept, and he wanted pictures to prove it. He still had over twenty-four hours until the kick-off and he planned to use this time to the best advantage in gaining a few priceless memories. Because they had both been wounded in the line of duty, he decided to take Ice Pick and Peanut with him to join his parents at the beach house he had rented for them. He told them to pack for an overnight trip and meet him at ten o'clock.

Peanut showed up with his backpack, skateboard, and a Mac 10 sub machine gun. Ice Pick knew better than to come armed, but he was wearing a flak jacket.

"Guys, I should have told you that dress was casual for this thing," Arthur said. "You'll scare the crap out of my parents. They are freaking out enough already."

Arthur hired a car from the service to drive them the hour up north to where his parents were staying. Arthur suggested that the three happy playmates sing songs along the way and the driver could video tape them. Ice Pick told him that it was a good thing that his weapons were in the trunk, or he'd shoot Arthur in the foot. He wasn't about to perform in a sing along, and he certainly wouldn't agree to have it documented on film—he had a reputation to uphold.

"I was just trying to think of something that normal kids would do on a car trip," Arthur explained as he turned his attention back to *The New York Times*.

The car pulled up to the gatehouse just before noon. Arthur gave the digital code for the gate and as it began to open Arthur's parents came running out of the small, two-bedroom gatehouse.

"What are you guys doing here?" Arthur asked.

"Ain't this the house you rented for us? This is the right address," Mr. Andrews answered.

"This is just the gatehouse to the compound. Before there were electronic gates the gatekeeper would live here. We're staying at the main estate up the driveway," Arthur explained.

He knew from reading *People* magazine that people like the royal family and the Kennedys spent their vacations at compounds, not houses. Arthur had rented this place from a prominent CEO who was now on trial for embezzlement.

"What's wrong with this place," his dad asked.

As far as Arthur could tell there was nothing wrong with the gatehouse, it just wouldn't look as impressive in the photographs he'd planned for later in the day. Even the imperious Arthur couldn't convince his mom and dad to move into the mansion a quarter of a mile down the driveway.

In the spirit of family cohesion, he decided to stay with them in the charming little cottage. Ice Pick and Peanut said that they wouldn't be caught dead in that dump and so they set up in the mansion by themselves. They kept themselves busy playing video games on the big screen TV and eating pizza while Arthur went about collecting the cherished memories of his fictional childhood.

After he settled in, Arthur came out to the porch to meet his parents. He was wearing white tennis shorts, a white cable knit cotton sweater, and canvas boat shoes. He looked like a fifth-grade male gigolo at Martha's Vineyard.

"We should take out the sailboat," Arthur said to his dad. "Mom can take pictures of us."

"I don't know squat about boats, neither do you. I should remind you that ain't both of us put together amount to much of a swimmer."

Mr. Andrews' syntax was immune to Arthur's derision, so Arthur had stopped correcting him long ago.

The truth was that the last thing Arthur wanted to do was go sailing, but he had seen pictures of the young royals boating. Arthur was absolutely positive that he would hate sailing, and now he wondered if the royal kids hated it too. Maybe everything they did sucked? Before he had come across those articles in the magazine describing the idyllic childhood of celebrities, he never had many complaints about his own. Maybe a youth devoid of memories of sailing didn't represent neglect?

Tennis, golf, badminton, horseback riding, water skiing, and all of the other leisure activities usually associated with the rich also seemed like a total bore to Arthur and his parents. Arthur and his mother settled back on the porch swing of the cozy gatehouse, both with a book. Over the years reading had been the one activity that Mrs. Andrews could enjoy with her son in silence. Arthur also seemed contented with this speechless quality time.

Mr. Andrews looked around the compound for a way to entertain himself. He scouted out the boathouse but passed up the jet ski and speedboat as frivolous—he had a rule of never trusting toys with internally combusted engines that would need to be repaired. He settled on a riding mower in the six-car garage and cut the grass on the whole estate. Arthur wondered if his father's choice of a pastime would rate him a discount on the rental of the mansion.

In the late afternoon on the porch of the gatehouse, Arthur and his parents sipped iced tea that Arthur had prepared himself from a recipe he found in *Town & Country*. For the first time Arthur explained to them the royal family envy that had infected him when he read the magazine article.

"That's why you got me wearing a suit, because of them little royal pansy asses?" Mr. Andrews asked. "You're picking a pretty lousy role model if you're trying to be like royalty. Pound for pound they's about the most worthless animals on the planet."

Mrs. Andrews shook her head in agreement with her husband.

"Son, they got to build mental hospitals and drug treatment facilities just to house them folks. Good grief, if you need to admire people you might as well look at the most-wanted posters down at the post office," Mr. Andrews laughed. "The way we's all brought up is pretty much a crap shoot as to how we's gonna turn out in the end."

Once he gave it a bit of consideration, Arthur realized hadn't really thought this through all the way. Historically speaking you'd have to go all the way back to Charlemagne to find a monarch who had actually achieved anything on his or her own merits—and Charlemagne was illiterate most of his life. In the modern era, our vestigial royalty had a completely shameful history. The same could be said for the progeny of much of our modern elite.

"I guess my whole strategy could use an overhaul," Arthur said as he reeled from this new epiphany. "I had a pretty good life before all of this," he said as he looked around at the trappings of the rich.

"You had it a lot better than your mother and I had it when we were your age." Arthur was slightly startled by his father's words until he decided that the proper pronoun and verb tense usage was completely an accident.

"I guess this means that I can shut down the casino and the sports betting operation," Arthur added.

"I guess I can go back to my old job in the service department," Mr. Andrews cheered. "I can save that suit for when you graduate from college,"

"Or maybe when I'm acquitted on my first insider trading conviction," Arthur added.

His parents had always encouraged him to aim for the stars.

Even Arthur's mother was feeling elated, just not so much that she felt a need to verbalize any of her joy.

"I guess that I can call off the rather gruesome retaliation I was going to rain down on that Digotti creep and his thugs," Arthur countered.

Mr. Andrews thought about that one for a second.

"Them the guys that kidnapped me and your mom the other night?"

"Precisely."

"Hang on a second, Arthur. Let's not be too quick to abandon all of your hard work. You spent a lot of time planning this thing, and besides, after what they done to us, maybe you need to teach them a little lesson."

"That will sure make my guys happy. They can live with closing the casino, calling off Operation Overkill would break their hearts."

***

The next morning Arthur, Ice Pick, and Peanut drove back home in a private car. Arthur had a few phone calls to make along the way and he didn't want to involve his parents in a criminal conspiracy by having them in the same vehicle. Kick off time, for the game and for Operation Overkill, would be at 6:30 Eastern Standard Time.

In his planning, Arthur had ignored all of the suggestions of the more pathological members of his organization. Slasher insisted that he could buy a few pounds of Semtex from a friend of his older brother in seventh grade. Rat Face offered the use of his extremely ill-tempered pit bull to help even the score with Digotti. Ice Pick came up with the idea to bribe the kitchen staff at the strip club to under-cook the chicken wings they were serving at the party. The *pièce de résistance* would be Arthur phoning in a huge bet under the name Sal Monela.

Because Arthur considered himself to be a very progressive employer, and because he wanted to encourage his staff's initiative, he gave them all bonuses for their ideas, but told them that he already knew a nonviolent way to punish the gangsters. It was a good thing that Arthur was dissolving his operation so that his crew could go back to playing little league baseball and video games. Childhood shouldn't be filled with work. As much fun as it had been, there would be plenty of time for jobs and careers.

An hour before game time, Arthur stopped taking bets and closed down his operation. He and his boys moved across town to the Deja-Vu and waited across the street in a surveillance van they had hired for the day. The strip club had four exits: the front entrance and three heavy steel fire doors that all opened out. Arthur had hired a Department of Transportation crew for the day who quickly placed heavy concrete barriers, called jersey walls, in front of all the doors to bar egress from the Deja-vu immediately after kick-off. Everyone inside would stay inside until they were rescued. It wouldn't be the Arthur's DOT crew doing the rescuing as they all went home to watch the game.

Being stuck inside a bar with plenty of food and beer for the Super Bowl seems more like where good people go when they die rather than retribution, but then came the second part of Arthur's plan. Frankie One Eye cut the satellite cable on the roof for all of the televisions inside. Sitting in the van across the street Arthur could hear the tortured howls inside the strip club. Arthur wasn't quite as marveled by his own cruelty at times like this when he saw how much his gang was enjoying this.

About the only people you can reach on the phone during the Super Bowl are pizza deliverers, and they wouldn't be able to move ten jersey walls, even if you gave them a really big tip. When someone inside called the police, they were told that help would come first thing Monday morning. The Deja-vu was a known organized crime hangout and the police could care less about their game-day problems. Arthur had one more move to make as he and his crew pulled away. He punched in Digotti's number.

"Digotti here."

"Mr. Digotti, Arthur Andrews here. I just wanted to tell you that you won."

"Wha?"

"I'm out of the business. I quit. I guess we're even now."

"Oh no. I'd say we're pretty far from even, you little puke. When I get out of here…"

Arthur cut him off.

"Before you do anything you will certainly regret, and you will regret it, let me fill you in on my insurance policy. Does the word "Goodfellas" mean anything to you?"

Silence.
"That's your email password."

"How'd you get that?"

"I also have your ATM PIN number and all of your online passwords—all of them some moronic variation of 'goodfellas.' I have a great picture of you that I photo-shopped wearing a French maid outfit that I'm thinking of posting on the web site for the Deja-vu. To put it mildly, the picture isn't very flattering. You just sit in the dark over there and check game scores on your phone. When someone lets you out, if someone lets you out, you had better forget all about me."

Arthur hung up in the middle of Digotti's string of abuse.

Arthur was well aware that men fear that which they do not understand. He knew that men like Mr. Digotti had no understanding of the computer world; to them it was like magic. It had taken the tech-impaired Digotti years to summon the courage to open an email account and any warning to destroy it would weigh heavier than a death threat. He wouldn't bother Arthur or his boys.

Arthur was dropped off at home just in time to watch the halftime show. His parents were watching the game together. Mr. Andrews had the coffee table in front of the TV loaded with his favorite snacks: chips, dip, mini pizzas, and domestic beer. As soon as Arthur had renounced his über-yuppie lifestyle Mr. Andrews threw out all the stuff in the fridge their son was making them eat. Mr. Andrews hoped that he'd never be forced to eat sushi, hummus, pâté, or caviar ever again. He hadn't been this happy and relaxed in months.

"Welcome home, son," Mr. Andrews said as Arthur walked in the room.

"Thanks, dad," Arthur replied. "How are you, mom?"

"I'm good, Arthur," Mrs. Andrews spoke.

"Yes, you are good, mom. You're very good."

Arthur sat down between them, put his feet up on the table, and watched the vulgar halftime entertainment with a relish that he imagined the people in magazines would envy.

THE GOLDEN GIRLS

"Look it up," Lonnie said. "An eye for an eye, everyone's read that, right? It doesn't stop there, though. It goes on and on. A hand for a hand, a foot for a foot. It says that right in the Bible, a foot for a damn foot."

"It doesn't say that."

Ray had always been the skeptic of the three.

"Google it, you think I'm lying."

"I ain't got no battery," Ray said, holding his mobile phone from the last days of the previous century.

"It's just the rules. Someone steps up to you, you got to step up to that punk. We need to mess this guy up. He embarrassed us."

Lonnie was the leader of this group. Ray and Hap wouldn't argue that fact, no one would. What no one could tell you is what he was leading them towards.

"Eye for a eye, yeah. Maybe even the 'foot for a foot' part, but no way does the Bible say you take an eight-ball for an eight-ball. There weren't no pool back when Jesus was around, and definitely no cocaine," Hap said.

Hap was the brains of the crew, which in this case wasn't the sort of honor you'd imagine of a criminal organization, although "criminal organization" were two words no one would use together to describe the doings of Lonnie, Ray, and Hap. As many times as they'd been in a courtroom, even the most rabid prosecutor wouldn't be able to keep a straight face declaring them a criminal organization.

Lonnie sent Ray over to the Happy Days Tavern near the docks with the cocaine to deliver to a kid they knew called Red Stallers. Ray handed over the package in what he thought was a deft hand-shake, but Red didn't reciprocate with the cash.

92

"Catch you later, granny."

Red strolled out of the bar leaving Ray in stunned silence thinking of that TV show with the four old gals.

"What was I supposed to do? Give him a beat down right there in Happy Days? I don't want to become *persona non grata*. I been going there since before I was even legal to drink."

Red Stallers was twenty-five and built like a pallet of bricks. Ray was sixty-six and asthmatic. Anyone expecting him to give Red a beat down would've been seriously delusional. Ray, by the way, was the "muscle" of the group, or was at one point in the mostly uneventful trajectory of their shared criminal activity across several decades.

Lonnie hadn't expected Ray to physically confront the young stevedore who could probably deadlift all three of them. It was up to him to resolve the issue. That's why he was the leader.

Lonnie had worked with Red's father on the Baltimore docks, way back, before he died of lung cancer when his son was in high school, so the kid had no male figure around to teach him manners, things like not stiffing his coke dealer.

The next evening, Lonnie sat next to Red at Happy Days.

"You owe us three hundred," Lonnie said.

Red laughed.

"You made us look bad. I can make you look worse."

"Fuck off, gramps."

"I'll forgive that crack because I knew your father, but a debt's a debt. You gotta pay."

Red returned to his beer.

"I got school records of you in seventh grade. Sent home for shitting your pants. The Freedom of Information Act opens up all those old files."

Red's dad had told Lonnie the story, not the sort of thing you'd ever forget.

Red sat up straighter on his barstool, suddenly very interested in the old guy on his right.

"I can almost excuse a kid in first grade, maybe second, but a seventh-grade kid crapping his pants? I'm sure you had a good reason that your pals will understand."

Of course, there were no records, but Red was as dumb as he looked and paid the crew the next day. The young stevedore druggy thug was a lousy Catholic, but he'd read Exodus.

An eye for an eye, an embarrassment for an embarrassment.

CHOW, AMIGOS

Chow? What the hell was that? Eduardo had heard of Purina Dog Chow from TV commercials as a kid. He knew a lot of words for "food" in English, even more in Spanish. Chow just seemed vulgar. He could think of a half dozen better words in French. He took three years in high school back in Texas instead of Spanish, which would've been a lot easier. He could already read and write Spanish better than the teacher and besides, French class had prettier girls, and not the same Latinas he knew since he was three years old.

His Tex-Mex friends who took Spanish never actually learned how to write it, but that didn't stop them from tagging school walls with half-literate nonsense, English phonetic spellings of basic Spanish words that sounded OK but looked like horrible scars when committed to the written word. Every time Eduardo saw one of those linguistic crimes, he felt like grabbing a can of red paint and marking it up like a teacher correcting a failed quiz. No one seemed to bother with accent marks in Spanish these days. The fact that he was above-average literate in Spanish and English was probably the only thing keeping him alive in lock-up. He had a niche position writing letters for other inmates to their friends, families, girlfriends, but mostly to their lawyers.

His job in the library was thought to be the best gig in the whole joint, and he didn't even have to join a gang to get it. Once again, they desperately needed someone who could read and write in both Spanish and English. It also worked highly in his favor that he was well-read. Most of the rank and file of the three Latino prison gangs spoke so little Spanish that they probably couldn't manage ordering in a Mexican restaurant, not even in the States. LINO, or Latino in name only, as Eduardo called them.

Working at the library meant he had access not only to the computer, but to the printer as well. And thus, his sideline of writing letters began. He wrote letters for dudes from the Latin Kings, Aryan Brotherhood, La Eme, Nazi Proud Boys, and the five different African-American gangs. He was an equal-opportunity wordsmith. No one would ever mess with Eduardo. Say you had a beef with him and beat his ass, but good. He misses a day at the library and can't write his letters. All those people who didn't get their letters that day are going to stomp you into dust, bro. Eduardo had become too big to fail. They called him the Scribe.

He was finishing what were the last months on a possession with intent charge. He'd pulled a year already and with good behavior he was almost assured early release in March. He just needed to keep clean and his head down, which he'd done since he entered the medium-level security facility. Technically, he wasn't supposed to be using the library printer except for official use, but he paid for all the copies he made at five cents apiece. He had receipts to prove it, not like anyone would come looking, but he couldn't take any chances as far as his prison record was concerned.

He didn't even take payment for his letters. He didn't smoke, do drugs, and he wouldn't touch the hooch they brewed in the cell block. He did all his work as "favors" meaning he did it for the protection, although this was never mentioned. He was more than happy with the transactions because no one inside so much as looked at him the wrong way. He kept to himself, at least when he wasn't working or handing out free legal advice to other cons. He'd never studied the law, not officially, but he read up on it in the library, and just from the endless amount of court dramas they all watched on the communal TV, he could at least talk a good game.

The old adage that you can't please all the people all the time was never truer than in prison. No matter how respected and useful Eduardo made himself among the general population, everyone had enemies. In his case, it was the miserable prick who ran the Nazi Proud Boys who blamed Eduardo for screwing up his last parole hearing.

Eduardo had written an eloquent defense of an indefensible asshole who wouldn't make parole any time before hell froze over, regardless of the poetry of any appeal made by the prisoner.

The passive-aggressive douche-bag didn't even have the nerve to let Eduardo know that he was unhappy with the product he'd been given for free, but Eduardo sensed that there was now bad blood between them. The Nazi wannabe fumed under the radar of the general population, waiting for his chance to get payback.

Eduardo just wanted to do quiet time and move on with his life. He had plans. But something was really getting under his skin lately, something besides the Nazi prick who didn't make parole.

Something Eduardo couldn't help noticing since his first day inside was how the inmates made things so much worse for themselves. He got it. Prison sucks, being locked up like an animal 24/7 with someone telling you when to do absolutely everything. But why did the inmates have to make it so much worse? The brutality, the senseless violence, the fighting over everything from a cigarette to an extra fruit cup, it didn't have to be that way. If everyone simply respected one another, things would be infinitely more bearable.

The Nazi was known as Buckshot by his boys and maybe even his own mother had called him that as a baby—which would explain a lot. Eduardo couldn't help thinking that even his name was repugnant and violent. Although Buckshot glared at him with hatred every single time they crossed paths, Eduardo thought the Nazi wouldn't dare make a move on him. Still, Eduardo didn't like that he had such a powerful inmate as an enemy.

He learned almost immediately that the violence and intimidation were simply forms of currency for the inmates, at least in their twisted set of rules. The con's code of respect was what drove about ninety-nine percent of the misery inside the walls of American penitentiaries. The only respect in this place came from fear, intimidation, and sadism. Eduardo thought it didn't need to be that way, but he gave up trying to do anything to change things. He'd gained the respect of a big part of the inmate population, and he did it without threats or violence, but few inmates had his marketable skill sets to keep them above water.

He had little worry about being shaken down by every sociopath in the place, like almost every other fish, or new inmate. He felt bad for prisoners who didn't have his exalted status, and he did what he could to mitigate circumstances when he was able, but he'd learned just to keep to himself and serve out his sentence. He even had a cell to himself these days. It was smaller than the others, but having his own cell was almost too good to be true, if you could even say that about life in a cage.

March. It was either a million miles away, or right around the corner, depending on how Eduardo chose to look at it. It would take him that long to finish reading the stack of World War Two history books he had on reserve in the library. Three months was nothing. Downhill all the way. Eighty-five days and a wake up, as they liked to say inside.

Because he worked in the library, he was one of the first inmates to enter the chow hall for lunch and dinner. He'd sit down at a different empty table every time, which would fill up with the cons who sat at that particular table every day, most of them affiliated with one gang or another. He wasn't exactly welcomed at every table, but nobody gave him any grief about it either. He'd either eat in silence, or make polite conversation, depending on the group.

On this day, it was dudes from the Latin Kings who felt Eduardo was one of their own, although they didn't know his heritage, they just figured he was Mexican from his first name. He spoke Spanish better than any of them, at least he was more grammatical, although his accent was a bit strange. His last name was Bellaguer, which didn't sound Mexican at all. So, the Latin Kings, like the other inmates, didn't know much about the Scribe.

"This chow is fucking disgusting, yo," said one of the Kings.

"How can you mess up *frijoles*?" another added.

Eduardo was going to just eat and leave, but they'd touched one of his recent nerves: prison food, or what passed for it.

"Everything on this tray comes out of a can. We sit here in the middle of California and the richest farmland on earth, and they never buy fresh? Unbelievable. They probably pay more to move out all of the trash created by the cans they empty than fresh vegetables would cost."

The other cons at the table looked at him, waiting for more. The few that knew anything about Eduardo knew that once he sunk his teeth into an issue, he didn't let go easily.

"Once again, cons cook our food. Why do they want to make life here worse than it already is by poisoning us with this…chow? Fuck, I can't even believe how much I hate that word. Chow? It just shows a complete lack of respect for what we put into our bodies. I wish I never had to hear that awful word again. I hate it almost as much as the food they serve us."

"Whadya gonna do?" one of the homies shrugged.

"I can cook. My folks ran a restaurant in L.A. My mom cooked for seven of us at home and we were poor, or poor-ish, at best. We never ate shit from cans, not much anyway. It's cheaper to eat good food than garbage, my mom always said. Canned pinto beans? She wouldn't ever think of that. She'd buy a big bag for two bucks, soak them over-night, and cook them the next day, enough for a few days, even in a big family."

Eduardo was on a roll.

"Canned green beans? Fucking stuff is a crime against food. Maybe frozen, in a pinch, but canned? You eat those six months after the world comes to an end from a nuclear war."

Eduardo's lecture-diatribe lasted ten minutes, until the guards cleared them out for the next round of cons waiting to eat.

As they took their trays to the racks, one of *jefes* of the Latin Kings took Eduardo aside.

"You can cook? Let me get you in the kitchen, bro."

Of course, Eduardo had no reason to leave his job at the library and all the privileges that came with it. Besides, the other inmates wouldn't allow it. But he could do a couple double shifts a week in the kitchen before his shift started in the library. It'd mean a lot less free time, but he leaped at the challenge.

On his first day in the chow hall kitchen, Eduardo talked with the other workers and articulated his hatred of the word "chow" and how it was part of the problem.

"First of all, we need to respect food, treat it for what it is: our sustenance. It's what keeps us alive. Without food, we die. It's an easy concept."

On his first day in the kitchen, he could only work with the ingredients at hand. Later, he could change the purchasing orders, he hoped. He started with the sauce for pasta. Instead of just dumping cans of tomato purée on top of over-cooked noodles, Eduardo showed them how to make tomato sauce with ingredients already available in the kitchen larder. Cans of whole tomatoes, cans of tomato purée, cans of tomato paste, all simmered with sautéed onions and garlic, seasoned with salt, basil, and red pepper flakes.

Not over-cooking the pasta was difficult when serving more than two thousand inmates, but the sauce was excellent, worthy of a decent restaurant.

The gen-pop, used to eating without thinking, couldn't help but notice the change in quality of the "chow" they'd just consumed. They didn't give the kitchen crew a standing ovation, but most of them sensed that the food was better than normal. The tomato sauce would be on the menu every Thursday. Not only was the sauce better than normal, but once inmates expected it and for any reason it wasn't served, there was a risk of a riot in the chow hall.

The chow hall had a new, modest addition, thanks to Eduardo's request. There was a chalkboard at the beginning of the line to announce the "Menu of the Day." It was a European affectation that Eduardo realized few inmates would appreciate, but he thought it went a long way to increase everyone's respect for what they were eating.

Eduardo harbored no dreams of turning the chow hall into a Michelin star dining facility, but he knew it wouldn't be difficult to improve both the taste and the nutritional value of what was prepared in the kitchen without spending more, and perhaps by spending even less. For example, beans of all types were much cheaper in the dried version than the cooked and canned variety.

One of the new inmates was talking with Eduardo in the library the next afternoon. He was a smart kid, in for a bullshit drug charge, like so many in this facility. He and Eduardo were talking about their favorite crime novels when Buckshot swaggered in and sat down at their table. Eduardo knew the Nazi well enough to know that he could barely read and only came into the library to intimidate him.

Eduardo stood up almost immediately and started placing books on a book rack with wheels, stuff requested by inmates who were confined to their cells for a variety of reasons. Buckshot gave the new kid a glare that practically made the newbie break out in hives. The kid got up and started to walk out.

"What's the hurry, pretty boy? Sit back down here."

The kid froze.

"What's your name?"

"Tony," the kid stammered.

"Why don't you read me a story, Tony?"

Buckshot couldn't get at Eduardo, so he'd threaten and terrorize people around the protected Scribe. Eduardo didn't even know this kid, didn't even know his name before, but now he felt responsible for his safety. His own personal hall-pass in the prison kept him protected but didn't include inmates around him. Buckshot wouldn't care that this kid and Eduardo weren't friends.

The Scribe had something Buckshot sorely lacked, which was empathy and compassion for his fellow inmates. After this one conversation that Eduardo shared with the kid, he'd now feel bad if Buckshot did something to him. This "something" could be beat or rape him, or even murder the young kid for no reason.

"Buckshot, can we talk? Just the two of us?"

The Nazi Proud Boy leader ignored Eduardo and kept making the newbie extremely uncomfortable with his tone of voice and demeanor, like he was chatting up a woman at a bar.

"Seriously, we need to talk. I have information for you on your parole review. Got it from someone inside."

This got the attention of the Nazi who sprang to his feet and put his face almost nose-to-nose with the Scribe. The newbie took the occasion to walk quickly out of the library.

"This better be real good, boy, and not just you cock-blocking me."

Of course, Eduardo had nothing new to tell the creep, except that anyone suspected of gang activity inside was rarely granted parole. It was about the only weapon the administrators had when it came to inmate anarchy. Eduardo needed to come up with some sort of bullshit to lay on the Nazi.

"They said that you lacked…what was the word they used?"

"Who?" Buckshot demanded.

"Sincerity. That was the word. Said you lacked sincerity."

"The fuck does that mean?"

"Means you need to be a better actor, that's all. The good news is you can work at it, practice it."

Buckshot wasn't bright by any stretch of anyone's imagination, but in this moment, he desperately wanted to understand.

"You mean like a movie actor?"

Jesus, he really was a fucking moron, Eduardo thought.

"Exactly! Who's your favorite actor?"

Buckshot didn't need a spilt-second to think.

"Steven Fucking Seagal."

Buckshot threw out a flurry of air punches and kicks in honor of his hero.

"So, you think Seagal doesn't have to practice playing his roles on film?" Eduardo asked, barely able to maintain his gravitas. "Fuck no, an actor of his caliber has to live the role, not just mouth the words in the script."

"Whadya mean 'live the role'?"

"I mean he has to act it out, night and day way before they even start filming."

"No shit?"

"No shit. You want the parole board to think you're walking the straight and narrow in here, you need to pretend like that's exactly what you're doing."

Eduardo really didn't know Buckshot well enough to know just how stupid he really was, but he was about to get a much better look into the mind of the heavily tattooed, barely-literate, racist asshole. Eduardo had nothing to lose while the gen-pop had a lot to gain from a less violent Buckshot.

"I just gotta pretend to be nice?"

"That's what they want."

"I ain't got another shot at a hearing for eight months."

"Time to start pretending."

Eduardo was astounded that Buckshot had even had a prayer at another parole hearing, everyone knew he didn't deserve it.

This was an interesting development for Eduardo to learn that the Nazi had hope. Hope was a good thing. Hope could be manipulated. Prison Nazi nihilism couldn't be manipulated, not for anything good at least.

This seemed like a good time to repair the bad blood that had come between them since Buckshot's failed parole hearing, although

Eduardo knew better than to mention that directly. He offered the Nazi his services once again as a letter writer. Buckshot just grunted and walked away. It was definitely one of his friendlier grunts, so Eduardo felt that progress had been made, a step forward.

From the few times when Eduardo spoke with Buckshot, back when he was trying to give him a hand with his last parole hearing, he decided that he was a moron, a moron and a virulent racist. He doubted if the Nazi would have even spoken with him face-to-face if Eduardo had a darker complexion. Almost everyone inside was racist to one degree or another; that's just how it was. Even for a guy whose every acquaintance had several swastika tattoos, Buckshot really seemed to over-do it on the racism.

Eduardo couldn't help but think that the loudest racists, the ones with the most hateful tattoos, were like the closet queens who antagonized the gay prisoners. The lady doth protest too much, was the first thought that ran through Eduardo's mind. Did he have a hidden Barack Obama tattoo somewhere on his meth-ravaged carcass? Had Buckshot fallen in love with a Mexican girl in the West Texas town of El Paso? He was a rather unrepentant Marty Robbins fan, after all. That's sort of like a queer-basher skipping around the cellblock whistling show tunes.

For the moment, Eduardo had bigger fish to fry, although the prison never served fish except of the stick variety that probably only contained trace elements of any sea-dwelling species. His next project, his next hurdle was to replace the canned beans the kitchen served with beans prepared from scratch.

"I thought we could try to make our beans from scratch instead of using this canned version," Eduardo said to the con kitchen manager who didn't even look old enough to be in prison.

"Why don't I order a few cases of live lobster while we're at it," Barney said. "I'll let you do the wine pairing."

Barney got to where he was in the kitchen hierarchy because he was smart and tough. He had no gang affiliation, yet no one ever messed with him. Eduardo learned that Barney basically did the job of three prison officials tasked with running the kitchen. They made it abundantly clear, through the guards and their influence with the gangs, that no one was to so much as look at Barney with anything less than total respect. Or else.

Or else what, Eduardo always wondered, at least until he started working in the kitchen. Most of the drugs and swag entering the prison came in with the food service orders. If any prisoner even made Barney uncomfortable, the swag would stop until the con was "educated" about his transgression.

Barney told Eduardo a story about just how deep his protection went in the prison.

"I was on a three-on-three game with ganged-up guys from the Black Guerilla Family. I took a pretty hard foul, but nothing too major. I didn't even call it; I took much worse fouls in intramural basketball at USC—and by the way, the frat boys in the league were my best customers," Barney said.

"Best customers for what?" Eduardo asked.

"Never mind. I guess you never heard why I'm in here."

Barney got back to his story.

"So, we kept playing, no problem, but a guard saw the foul and sent the info upstairs. The next day, the Black Guerilla Family made their guy apologize to me, no shit. Embarrassing, to be honest."

Eduardo pressed the de facto kitchen manager on the beans.

"I've done the math on this. We'll save money buying dried beans, like forty-five percent a month."

"Sorry if I don't take your word for it, Eduardo," Barney said.

The young kitchen worker immediately looked up this preposterous suggestion in his purchasing catalogue on his tablet supplied by the civilian manager.

"OK," he said, looking at the figures. "But who's gonna cook them? Me?"

Eduardo didn't have time to reply before Barney clarified this point.

"I can't cook a damn thing. I work in the kitchen because I can do math, something the civilian managers can't, evidently, or won't."

"You like some great entrepreneur?" Eduardo asked.

"Got kicked out of USC business school for selling drugs," Barney said. "My full ride didn't include the BMW I drove."

Eduardo shook his head in understanding.

"I cook beans. I'll walk your people through it. It's the easiest thing in the world. Why do you think Mexicans live on them?"

Barney raised his hands in the air.

"Because of centuries of tradition?" he asked, throwing up a Hail Mary.

"Because they're cheap and easy."

Barney was far from bowled over by the idea, but he acquiesced.

"OK, but if the cons don't like'em, I'm going to make you eat every last one of those damn beans."

Eduardo could cook beans as well as the next guy who'd grown up in a Mexican restaurant, but he was baffled by the scale of cooking for 2,300 inmates. It was time to learn, he thought as he threw the first twenty pounds of dried pinto beans in a plastic barrel to soak for twenty-four hours. That was his first trick. Instead of just an overnight soak, his mother had taught him to allow the beans to soak, then let them sprout.

The first batch Eduardo boiled in the 60-gallon caldron with sautéed onions, garlic, and carrots. He added only salt and pepper for seasoning, not wanting to challenge the intestinal tracts of the inmates by throwing in spicy chiles. He was even given some meat scraps and a few bones to add to the broth.

The beans were a resounding success, at least for the fraction of inmates who sampled them before they ran out. Eduardo would've liked to serve the beans with corn or flour tortillas, but one thing at a time. The diners would have to settle for a slice of white bread with a tab of margarine.

It turned out that not serving the first batch of beans with tortillas was a stroke of luck as this would have made the meal way too ethnic for the Nazis, or at least one Nazi. Buckshot had overheard one of the cons call the beans "*frijoles*" that weren't even on offer by the time he made it through the line.

"Free-ho-lees? What the fuck they doing making Mexican food? This is America, God damn it." He shouted to his acolytes at the Nazi table.

Prison was even more rigid than high school as far as cafeteria seating went. You ate with your tribe, everyone except Eduardo who was sitting at the Muslim Brotherhood table minding his own business when he overheard Buckshot at the opening of his rant.

Luckily, Buckshot's attempt at pronouncing a Spanish word was so off-base that the Mexican gangs had no idea what the Nazi was screaming about.

"Fuck free-ho-lees. That ain't food for a white man to eat."

His rant became louder and more incomprehensible and insane with every word. Eduardo felt that his new rapprochement with the Nazi shot-caller allowed him to address him mid-rant.

"They're pinto beans. It's something everyone eats."

Buckshot stopped shouting, more out of astonishment that he'd been interrupted than a desire to listen.

"This is on me, Buckshot. I'm trying to make our food here healthier."

"Beans ain't even healthy."

"In fact, they are one of the healthiest foods convicts can eat," Eduardo said, emphasizing the species that everyone in the chow hall could claim as their own, even Buckshot.

The Nazi stood standing but was obviously waiting for Eduardo to continue.

"A single cup of pinto beans yields two-hundred forty-five calories, one gram of fat, forty-five grams of carbohydrates, fifteen grams of fiber, and fifteen grams of protein, which at less than one dollar a pound, that works out to be the most nutritionally significant food that comes out of this kitchen."

Buckshot and everyone else in the chow hall remained completely silent.

"I just memorized that this morning, but it's true. You can call them '*frijoles*' or 'beans' or whatever you want, but we'll all be better off eating more of them."

Buckshot sat down.

"I didn't even get none," he complained.

It was all Eduardo could do to keep from play-acting a bawling child who dropped his ice cream on the sidewalk.

"And for that, I sincerely apologize. I promise that there will be enough for everyone the next time these come up on the menu."

"When's that?" Buckshot asked while many other inmates were obviously thinking the same thing.'

"Soon."

Without really trying, Eduardo had turned a possible race riot into Nazi, Black, and Latino gang members all drooling over the thought of a good plate of *frijoles*, maybe even with tortillas.

Two days later, as they both waited in line for pasta with the new and insanely well-received tomato sauce, Eduardo edged a few places in line to talk to Buckshot.

"How old are you?"

Eduardo already knew how old the Nazi was as he bragged about his age and how he could still do ten clean pull-ups out in the yard.

"Fifty-eight."

"Fifty-eight. Let's see. Ever seen the TV show *Good Times* with Jimmy Walker?"

Buckshot tried to stonewall, but Eduardo pressed him.

"That was before my time, but I've seen every episode on the internet. You never watched it?"

"I seen it a couple times," Buckshot confessed sheepishly.

"That was on back when you were in what, junior high? Back when you were just entering puberty, right?"

"Fuck if I know. Told you I only seen it once or twice."

"See, I found that show on the internet when I was like fifteen years old. Even with all of the porno on the web when I was growing up, I must have jerked off to his sister on that show about a million times. No joke, I think I counted."

Buckshot chuckled.

"What the hell was her name on the show? Don't tell me, I know it. Tanya, Tara…"

"Thelma," Buckshot said.

"Thelma. Yes, thank you. Oh my God, she was such a goddess. She had the most beautiful ass I've ever seen, no joke."

"Bitch did have an ass on her," the Nazi admitted.

"So, here's something maybe you can explain to me about Nazis. You say that Blacks and other races aren't humans, right?"

"That's right, they's like animals."

"See, I don't get that. You ever jerked off thinking about an animal before?"

"I'm about to jerk off on your fucking dead body, my man," Buckshot said.

Eduardo couldn't help laughing at this.

"Fair enough, but just making a point. But if you can tell me to my face that you didn't jerk off thinking about Thelma's heavenly ass at least once, I'll get a swastika tattoo right now, let you do it. I'll preach all of your racist rhetoric, too."

Buckshot threw Eduardo a murderous glance, then broke out in laughter.

"I may have touched myself a few times inappropriately as I considered the fine Thelma."

"And are you going to tell me that Beyoncé isn't just completely fine?"

"I'll take the fifth," Buckshot pleaded.

"How about J Lo?"

"She ain't Black."

"Whatever, a woman of color," Eduardo said.

"Boy, I jerked off to underwear ads in Montgomery Ward catalogues back in the day, so that don't mean shit."

"Racial purity loses to testosterone once again. Hate the race, love that ass!"

"You can be an annoying piece of shit sometimes, Eduardo."

Buckshot started for his usual table.

"*Bon appétit*," Eduardo said in parting.

"Speak fucking English, God damn it. I hate Spanish."

"We say *buen provecho* in Spanish."

"Why's you always using foreign words?"

"Yeah, it's funny but we really don't have a way to say that in English."

"Maybe it's cuz our food ain't no good here."

"*Touché.*"

Buckshot started to crack a smile but stopped himself, like suppressing a sneeze.

"How'd you say 'asshole' in Spanish?" Buckshot asked.

Eduardo laughed out loud, and Buckshot smiled like he'd just won a bet.

Not everything they made in the kitchen was miserable, and there was only so much budgeted for food, so Eduardo knew to manage his expectations. His goal was to actually spend less and make more nutritious items. His next move was to include more fresh vegetables in the daily meals. He began with the least expensive fresh vegetables available to the prison: carrots, onions, and green beans.

These three had always been staples in the chow hall, but the problem, as Eduardo saw it, was that they cooked the life out of them. He proposed that they blanch the beans and carrots for only a couple minutes in boiling, salted water, and then throw them in an ice bath to stop the cooking process. These blanched vegetables would be added to the raw onions that had been sliced and macerated in vinegar. This was served as a cold salad.

As Eduardo had anticipated, this wasn't exactly an overwhelming favorite among the inmates, but he knew that it was a much healthier version than the previous over-cooked mush.

With his tomato sauce, pinto beans, and vegetable medley, Eduardo was satisfied that he'd not only raised the nutritional value of the prison fare, but he'd also improved the psychological well-being of the inmates. Maybe. Maybe not. No one really seemed to notice, but Eduardo already had a secure position of status with his letter writing operation. His work in the kitchen would also almost assure the approval of his parole when it came up for review in March.

He'd already arranged to live with his mother upon his release until he became solvent financially while he worked in her restaurant. Considering that he'd been an absolute model prisoner, along with all of the volunteer work he did to help fellow inmates, the members of the parole board would probably chauffer Eduardo personally to his mother's home directly after the hearing.

If Eduardo had a nickel for every time he'd written the words "Dear Honorable Members of the Parole Board," he'd could probably bribe his way out of this hellhole. For many of his clients, trying to make them look like real human beings to the board was one of the great challenges of his young life. Painting a turd, was the expression that came to mind when he worked with guys like Buckshot and other sociopaths. He tried to console himself with the idea that they all deserved a fair hearing. Besides, it was usually the case that the worse the inmate, the more they had to offer him in the way of protection.

The recent news in the cellblock was that Quique Martínez, the Latin Kings' boss had passed his parole hearing. Of course, Eduardo had penned his letter to the board, not that in itself had been enough to tip the scales of justice in favor of the notorious gangster. Everyone knew that, everyone except Buckshot who was blind with rage, rage he directed vociferously at the Scribe.

Eduardo received word about Buckshot's displeasure almost immediately. He was also assured by the Latin Kings that they had his back, and front, and sides. Still, Eduardo wasn't completely at ease knowing that he was on the shit list of the Nazi Pretty Boys' shot caller.

"Fuck that Nazi prick," Quique said. "He ain't coming nowhere near you."

Eduardo didn't think that Buckshot would make a move on him, and he appreciated that he was backed by such a powerful man in the cellblock. However, he'd feel better talking directly to Buckshot rather than relying on the Latin Kings to watch over him every minute out of lockdown.

Prison beefs ending in murder were often over the most childish, inconsequential matters: a stolen bag of corn chips, some sort of presumed disrespect, or an off-hand insult of a professional sports team. Buckshot's complaint about Eduardo's lack of vigor in his letter to the parole board was unfounded and unfair, but Eduardo had to admit that if Buckshot really felt that he'd been slighted, it was a serious matter, and he took the shot-caller's threats seriously.

Wednesdays at four in the afternoon, Eduardo gave a lecture on writing which attracted only five inmates in a classroom made for five times that many students. Although Eduardo tried not to let the poor attendance dampen his enthusiasm, his heart sprung when he saw three new faces enter the room until he recognized that they were part of Buckshot's crew who followed in after them.

Eduardo backed up to the chalkboard while his students pushed up against the opposite wall.

"Welcome to writing for your life, gentlemen," he said failing in his effort to sound unafraid.

"We ain't here for your faggot writing class, Eddy," Buckshot said, knowing Eduardo didn't like anyone calling him anything but Eduardo. "I just need you to tell me why you can spring that Latin Kings asshole while I get rejected again."

Just as he finished speaking, seven other inmates entered the classroom, five of them stopping directly behind Buckshot's men.

Oso was as big as a doorway and covered with nightmarish tattoos that told the story of a life spent behind bars. Without a doubt, the most feared man in the entire prison, guards included. One of Buckshot's boys had a plexiglass shiv in his sleeve, but thought better of pulling it out—going at Oso with a piece of sharpened plastic was like a rabbit attacking a real bear. Buckshot gave his men a look and they stepped back.

"So, you here to mess up our boy?" Oso asked. "Eduardo's a good kid. Why the fuck you think you need to do him?"

Oso stepped closer to Buckshot.

"Oso, chill. We're just talking," Eduardo said, desperately trying to avoid a homicide in his classroom. "It's cool."

"That ain't what we been hearing. He says he wants to do you, *hermano*," Oso said.

Oso pointed his finger at Buckshot which was as intimidating as a samurai sword.

"Can't let that happen, Hitler-loving motherfucker."

"Oso, man, it's cool between us, I swear. He was just talking some shit, didn't mean it."

"Don't matter. He said it and you're with us. Can't let this pass."

Eduardo, an astute pupil of the game of chess, was thinking a few moves ahead and could see that if he begged for the Nazi's life, Buckshot would resent him even more, so skewed was prison logic.

"Whatever beef I have with Buckshot, I can settle it myself."

Oso may have been the biggest man in the prison, but very little of his mass seemed to contain functioning brain matter. He was like a guided missile that Quique sent to destroy, but like a boomerang would return. What Oso wasn't programmed to do was reason with someone like Eduardo who he feared because of his intellect. Eduardo had helped Oso's family in their naturalization process where they lived in Texas, and he felt almost as much loyalty towards the Scribe as to his gang.

Oso backed up a step and lowered his steel.

"*¿Eduardo, estás seguro?*" Oso asked, his English failing him in this minor crisis.

"I'm sure, *hermano*. Don't worry about me."

Eduardo wasn't quite so sure of this and he was greatly relieved when Oso marched Buckshot and his men out of the classroom so that he could continue with his lecture. He'd deal with the shot-caller at another time after thought this through.

Three days later, Eduardo sent word that he wanted to talk with Buckshot at his convenience. The library was a good spot, Eduardo thought, as it was a very public place. There was also the menace of violent retribution if anything happened to the Scribe in his own domain, a small area with its modest collection of books, three tables, and the librarian's desk.

This was, or course, if Buckshot came alone as he'd promised.

Buckshot rambled into the library the following afternoon with two of his thugs and no representative of the Latin Kings to be found.

Eduardo stood up from his desk and motioned towards one of the empty tables. The two thugs stood blocking the door while Buckshot ambled slowly over to the table as if to announce how little he cared for talk.

"So, you get some spic off on parole who prolly ain't even a fucking American, but you can't hook me up when I needed you?"

"Do you have any idea of how hard Martínez worked on his fiction? He had everyone in the fucking joint here saying that he was a better dude than Jesus of Nazareth. What did I tell you before? You have to work on this, manage your PR, your public relations."

Buckshot didn't respond.

"I also told you I could help with that, and I meant it."

"Just how do I do that, Mr. Scribe?" Buckshot sneered.

Eduardo wanted to scream at him that the gang leader needed to at least make some sort of effort to be a real human being, instead of a violent and possibly murderous psychopath. Of course, he didn't say anything like this because as well-connected as Eduardo was these days, he couldn't survive a full-frontal attack from one of the prison's most violent gangs.

"They need to see you do something positive, something that benefits everyone. I would never tell you how to conduct business, but you need to have something, and it doesn't have to even be the truth, but something that says you're making an effort to improve not only your life, but of those around you."

"I take good care of my people."

"Eh, I'm not sure that rewarding your guys for stomping anyone you point out would be something worthy of demonstrating to the board."

Buckshot seemed to be trying to conjure up something, anything he'd done that could be considered a good deed.

"You have another hearing in August, right?"

"September."

"Great, you got seven solid months to work something out."

"Like what?"

Eduardo was relieved that this had moved from a possible assassination to a brain-storming session with the Nazi half-wit, if that wasn't entirely redundant.

"Let's talk about food."

"Huh?" Buckshot grunted.

"What is your favorite dish, for starters. Is there anything you miss from your childhood? Something that brings back good memories?"

Eduardo guessed that this tattooed monster probably had few good memories from his youth.

"I remember them boxes of mac and cheese I'd make after school. Man, them was good."

Comfort food, but on an almost toxic level, Eduardo thought. The box version of this dish came with poor quality noodles and a packet of chemicals that didn't include a single molecule of real cheese. Still, Eduardo thought this was definitely something to work with.

"Good choice, *Monsieur* Buckshot."

"Fuck your funny words."

"Just deferring to your remembrance of a culinary past."

Before Buckshot could lash out again, Eduardo beat him to the punch.

"Those are all English words; I fucking swear to you," Eduardo said, slightly rattled.

This time, Buckshot laughed.

"I gotta take your word on that."

Although he had nothing to do with the process, it was his idea. Buckshot's Mac and Cheese was insanely successful among the inmates when it came out of the kitchen a week later. Why wouldn't it be, Eduardo thought. It was an American classic, an institution in homes and restaurants for generations, yet few people had tasted an even moderately decent version of the dish. For the kitchen, it was something of a budget-buster and would only be offered twice a month.

On the days when it was served, the chalkboard at the head of the line announced, "Buckshot's Mac n' Cheese." Prison had changed Eduardo in many ways, so he didn't question why it filled him with such joy to see a Nazi pleased to see his name associated with what had become the prison's most requested dish.

Eduardo was granted parole in March, but his parole eligibility date was three months later. He was grooming the kid, Tony, to take over for him in the library and to be the new prison scribe. He was a smart kid and Eduardo hoped he'd receive the respect and protection he'd enjoyed during his term.

He worked in the chow hall up until his release. Buckshot had transferred into the kitchen, even though it was a less prestigious post than his old job in the wood shop, but he'd fallen in love with cooking, going so far as to see it as a possible profession if he was granted his parole. Hope was working some strange magic on the elder statesman of racism and violence. Eduardo still had grave doubts concerning Buckshot's transformation, but you never know, he thought.

One thing less flexible than Buckshot's demeanor was the prison slang. Even though the food had improved considerably, everyone still called it chow. He didn't want to hear that word ever again, even when it was about feeding cats and dogs.

Saying goodbye was a wretched thing in prison and no one enjoyed it, so it was mostly avoided at all cost. Saying goodbye drove home the point that everyone else was staying put in the worst place anyone could imagine.

Eduardo simply gave a salute to everyone in the kitchen as he headed back to his cell for the last time and then out-processing.

"Have a good life, Buckshot," he said.

It was just one of those stock phrases that inmates said to each other when one of them was heading out the door, with any luck, never to return.

Then Buckshot said one more thing that wasn't common at all, especially for him.

"*Bon voyage, hermano.*"

DIVERSITY HIRE, MY ASS

Juan Rodríguez considered himself an American, not Mexican-American. He was born in Texas and lived his entire life in the United States except for his deployments to Iraq and Afghanistan as a soldier in the U.S. Army. He felt the fact that he was bilingual didn't diminish, dilute, or enhance his status as a U.S. citizen. He'd voted in every election—local, statewide, and national—since he turned eighteen. He began working before he was legally allowed by law to work yet paid taxes and then paid into social security since he began his first formal job at fourteen. Anyone who tried to contend that he was somehow less of a citizen because his parents had come to America outside of legal channels was going to lose that argument, at least if Juan were party to the discussion.

He'd been a DEA special agent for five years, serving first in Seattle after his training, and then Miami. His features were more European than Mexican which was an advantage in undercover work where he was able to pose as Spanish, Moroccan, South American, or a dozen other nationalities. He was a gifted linguist and could mimic just about any Spanish accent from Castilian, to Cuban, to the *porteño* lilt of Buenos Aires. His French was just passable, but he could speak Spanish with a French accent and could pass for a Parisian or North African when dealing with Latin Americans who spoke no French, or at least not as well as Juan.

He also possessed in abundance the most important quality necessary for undercover work: he had nerve, balls, *cojones*. Perhaps he was born with this virtue or perhaps it was something he learned during six years in the infantry, much of it in combat in some of the most contested spots in America's Middle East wars. His combat experience also guaranteed that he knew his way around dozens of different small arms, as well as light artillery and explosives.

His personal evaluation reports were the highest granted at DEA and no one who worked with Special Agent Juan Rodríguez had anything but glowing things to say about him.

On a personal level, he tended not to socialize much with his coworkers. He didn't golf or play softball, the two big sports at the Miami DEA office. He wasn't anti-social, by any means, he simply had friends who weren't agents. Not being one of the boys, along with his success as a new agent tended to breed some resentment among the ranks. It also meant he often didn't have someone to defend him when his name came up in conversations behind his back.

Miami had not too long ago been the most prestigious of the DEA offices, but trafficking had shifted. El Paso was now where every special agent wanted to be, at least those with ambition, or, in Juan's case, those who needed to be near the action. He applied for a transfer when he was first eligible, and was immediately selected, leap-frogging over other candidates with twice as much time on the job. No one who worked with Special Agent Rodríguez or who supervised him had any doubt that he was qualified for the transfer to Fort El Paso, as the office was called among DEA agents.

Rodríguez worked several cases with another young agent in Miami and was as close to a friend as he had there among the DEA staff. They trained martial arts together in their off time and were drinking buddies. Not that Juan really needed it with his coworkers, but Jenkins had his back. So, when Jenkins overheard three agents mention Juan's transfer to the coveted El Paso office, he eavesdropped at a discreet distance.

"He's a fucking diversity hire. Christ, I wish I had two Mexican names," one of them said.

"Why not change it? You can be Roberto…what is Miller in Spanish?" another asked.

"It would be *molinero*, numb nuts," Jenkins said, interrupting the trio.

The three were embarrassed that they'd been caught in their bad-mouthing of a fellow special agent, something looked upon very unfavorably at the DEA.

"Was it a diversity move when he got his Distinguished Service Medal, Afghanistan Campaign Medal, and his Global War on Terrorism Expeditionary Medal? Not that he needed a boost from those to make the cut here. He was second in his class at Quantico. Oh, and he received a Bronze Star for an operation in Afghanistan. Any of you boys have a Bronze-fucking-Star?"

Of course, none of them had.

"Me neither, but I'm not a diversity hire."

The more Jenkins spoke, the angrier he became.

"I've heard the three of you speaking Spanish, and all three together wouldn't amount to a decent junior high Spanish teacher, not even a fucking substitute. Or maybe you don't think Spanish is important in this job?"

As the three agents made mealy-mouthed appeals about what they'd said before, attempting to back down from their insult, Jenkins continued his assault.

"Any of you blue-bloods think you could match Juan on the pistol range, or know as much as he does about small arms of every variety? And forget about hand-to-hand combat. I train with him regularly. He's been doing jiu-jitsu since he was a teenager. I don't consider myself a slouch on the mat, but I've never beat the guy, not one fucking time. I feel like a five-year-old fighting his father when I roll with him."

It wasn't that Jenkins had nothing but praise for his friend. Juan drank too much, but who among them didn't? Jenkins was also ex-military, an organization practically built around functional alcoholism. He knew that Juan was never going to be the career man who works his way up through the ranks to eventually run the show, or at least a big piece of it. Those posts were reserved for family men, careerists at heart. As far as Jenkins could tell, Juan didn't even like his job.

They had many conversations at the bar about their work. In Juan's estimation, the entire drug interdiction idea was a lie. Everything they did at DEA was doing nothing to curb the influx of illegal drugs into the United States.

"Sooner or later, we'll just legalize everything. I say, the sooner, the better," Juan had said. "What does this say about all the people we've put in prison so far?"

Juan liked working under-cover, he got off on the danger. It was his way of dealing with his PTSD from too much time spent in war zones. He confessed all of this to Jenkins. Even though he knew that Juan didn't believe in his work, he wasn't about to let these three blue-blood douche bags tear into his friend.

"You guys really want to go to the El Paso office?" he asked. "Be careful what you wish for."

The three "blue-bloods" had nothing to say.

"Special Agent Juan Rodríguez a diversity hire?"

Now he was fuming. Jenkins almost spat out his closing remark.

"Diversity hire, my ass."

*Juan Rodríguez is one of the protagonists in John Scheck's novel, *La Frontera Saga*.

GRAVEYARD SHIFT

Starting work at midnight was a cruel joke, an obscenity, and a circadian abomination that was called the graveyard shift. Like police departments everywhere, Seattle had three rotations: days, swings, and mids. Days went from 08:00 to 16:00, swings from 16:00 to 24:00 and mids from 00:00 to 08:00. Officer Pamela Bolton always had a problem answering the mundane question, "How was your day?" when her shift began at midnight and ended when normal people were leaving to begin their jobs.

It was the absolute worst duty you could pull in the Seattle Police Department, perhaps among the worst jobs you could do anywhere for anyone. If you were new to the force, you'd better get used to it because that was going to make up a good part of your life, whether you were a night owl or a morning person. If you screwed up, you were saddled with nights. Shit runs downhill, as the veterans were quick to point out. Rookies and fuck-ups were up to their eyelids in the shit at the bottom of the hill.

There was another old saying—especially among cops—that nothing good ever happened after two o'clock in the morning. Just seeing someone out walking at four o'clock in the morning was enough to arouse suspicion. Cops couldn't help but assume these people were up to no good, or they'd already committed a crime and were fleeing the scene.

The graveyard shift was mostly about dealing with drunks and drug addicts. Bars closed at two a.m. in Seattle, meaning there was a steady stream of shaky drivers heading east across the bridges to the suburbs, like rats scurrying away from a sinking ship—most people who lived in the city just stumbled home drunk on foot or took a taxi. Bolton thought that if she never made another DWI arrest in her career, it would be too soon, but she also knew that there was no getting around it. People were completely stupid about their ability to drive, no matter what. When she pulled someone over, she always asked them the same thing, at least she did after two o'clock.

"How much have you had to drink?"

Cops always framed the question so that it was incriminating. They didn't ask, "Have you been drinking?" because you could just say you weren't. It was sort of like that old trick question, "When did you stop beating your wife?" You couldn't win.

If you said that you'd only had one drink, she'd ask how big it was.

The correct answer to the question "How much have you had to drink?" was "Would you like to see my license and registration?" The correct answer, one that every cop, every prosecutor, and any defense lawyer worth a shit knew was that you kept your mouth shut except to give your name.

Only a complete moron would consent to a field sobriety test, even a stone-cold-sober moron. No one but some circus freak can say the alphabet backwards or stand on one leg and touch a finger to their nose. You can never pass that test, not if the cop doesn't want you to, and then it's her word against yours. Good luck with that.

Because misery loves company, they gave you a partner on the graveyard shift. The thinking was two cops could keep each other awake. The big, deep, dark secret was that having a partner meant taking turns sleeping. One cop could sleep while making the rounds, or you could park somewhere, way the hell out of the way, where both of you could sleep, but Bolton heard a lot of bad things happening to those sleep-deprived pairs.

If you were lucky, it would only be other cops fucking with you, like take the air out of all of your tires and then hit their siren and lights. She'd heard that story when she first got out of the academy and didn't know whether to believe it or not. Cops could be total assholes when it came to practical jokes. She'd heard of even worse pranks that she actually could confirm.

Another time, some teenager shot video of two cops passed out in the front seat of their cruiser. Filmed them for over a half an hour before he screamed for help at the top of his lungs, and then filmed the hilarious hijinks of the two cops waking up in a total panic. That story is most definitely true, and the video is still up on the internet. The two cops and their jobs with SPD separated not long after the video was uploaded.

Bolton was paired often with Dale Hendricks and they worked mids together every third cycle for the summer. Sleeping on the job was something Bolton wouldn't have considered for a split second, not under normal circumstances, with "normal circumstances" meaning a day job. She always worked hard at everything she'd ever done, but these hours were wearing her down. She didn't even feel safe driving during the night shift.

Hendricks had night patrols in Afghanistan where inattention to detail could result in death, or worse, the death of your squad members. That was duty. He almost quit early in his career as a Seattle cop after pulling his third straight cycle of "mornings," the new SPD euphemism for the graveyard shift. The term "mids" was banished, like that would solve the problem, just like calling people "homeless" instead of "bums" had solved so many problems.

No matter what you called the graveyard shift, Hendricks had never been more sleep-deprived in his life. He felt as logy and out of it as the meth-heads he was forced to rattle every day before the sun rose in the Pacific Northwest sky.

He'd read dozens of studies showing that staying awake at night screws up more than one hundred proteins in the blood, effecting blood sugar, energy metabolism, and immune function. The bottom

128

line is that it's detrimental to your health, which meant his job was basically killing him.

His new partner had three years in. Pamela Bolton was also a U.S. Army veteran and a good cop, as far as Hendricks could tell. She was married, but was living separately after she filed for divorce. Her husband was also on the force, a twelve-year veteran with a reputation as a hard-ass and a ball buster, with half a dozen complaints of excessive force filed against him, although he was never disciplined formally.

Pamel admitted on their first night out that mids were killing her.

"I don't sleep during the day. Just can't do mids. Does that make me a bad person?"

Hendricks couldn't sleep during the day, at least not for more than an hour or two. Nothing worked. He covered his windows with black construction paper. He wore ear plugs. Listened to songs of the whales on low volume.

"I even tried meditation, for Christ's sake!" he confessed.

Bolton had the same complaints, had tried the same remedies.

"So, what the fuck do we do about it" she asked.

They decided to sleep during their shifts, taking turns while one of them passed out in the passenger seat, the other drove or stayed awake while they parked.

This wasn't anything original in the history of night shifts, something both cops knew too well, but they swore they'd be smart about it, they wouldn't ever get caught. Getting caught seemed unlikely, and how hard could sleeping on the job be when you were always so close to nodding off at any minute during your shift? It was a simple matter of letting yourself go.

The new partners dubbed their plan "Operation Clean Living" because every plan needed a name, at least for military people. On their first shift Hendricks slept a solid three hours and felt like a newborn baby the following day. Bolton also confessed to a new state of consciousness.

At first, one of them would drive while the other slept, but they quickly discovered that they slept longer and more peacefully when the car was parked. This presented considerably more risk of getting caught, but the benefits outweighed the downside. The problem was that when they were parked, it was extremely difficult for the other person to stay awake.

They parked in places that were well protected against detection. They chose industrial areas along Marginal Way going towards the airport. These were abandoned after-hours and they thought they could hear another vehicle approaching, even if they were both asleep.

There were three crews at SPD that worked revolving shifts of six days on, then three days off. It was a good deal if you did the math as it gave you sixteen extra days off a year compared to the people working Monday-Friday days permanently. No matter how good of a deal the extra days off were, mids sucked. On their fourth day into their first mids cycle under Operation Clean Living, Hendricks and Bolton both slept four hours during their shift.

The transformation was remarkable. After their shifts, they'd go home and sleep another three or four hours with the rest of the day off until they returned at midnight.

"I feel like I just recovered from a chronic illness," Hendricks admitted to his partner on their fifth shift into Operation Clean Living.

It didn't even feel risky to either of them. They'd sometimes miss a radio call, but that was easily explained with a host of excuses from poor reception to dealing with a citizen. They didn't do the park-and-snooze routine every night, but they decided that the last day of the cycle would be a great time for it so that they could go into their three-day break as rested as they could be, especially if it was a weekday morning when there wasn't much happening in the Emerald City.

Without any prodding on his part, Pamela told Hendricks about her failed marriage. He really wasn't interested, especially since she was still married to the guy, and he was a Seattle cop who outranked him. Hendricks didn't know the guy, never actually met him, but he knew who he was, had seen him around. The department was big, but not that big. There were about 1,400 officers, so it was like a medium-size high school.

After Bolton began filling his ear with stories about TJ, he asked around about the Charlie Crew sergeant. Maybe he'd asked all the wrong people, but no one had anything good to say about him. One of Hendricks friends from the academy who worked under TJ told him the guy was "a huge asshole." Said he fucked everything that moved including female officers under his supervision, along with hookers, strippers, barmaids, anything.

According to Bolton, he was also insanely jealous and had constantly accused his wife of infidelity. The jealous philanderer was such a cop cliché, Hendricks thought. If he had advice for any woman, it would be they should never, under any circumstances date a cop. He didn't know if female cops represented the same percentage of damaged goods as their opposite gender.

Hendricks was aware that what he possessed with what a sociologist would call anecdotal evidence, but he was amazed at how many of his fellow police officers were toxic when it came to relationships. TJ Albright was Exhibit A in this group, at least from what his wife had to say about him.

Hendricks had told Bolton that she shouldn't talk to her husband about what they were doing on their shifts together. They were quite literally sleeping together, at least at the times they weren't taking turns. He asked her if her husband had asked about him. He imagined that any insanely jealous misogynist would have something against a man their wife worked with for eight hours a day, or night, even if their relationship was on the outs. She said she wasn't speaking with her ex, not even a hello in the corridors.

"I'll only talk through my lawyer."

From what Bolton told him during their long shifts together, she'd never filed a complaint against her husband, and there was nothing in the department records about the physical abuse he inflicted on her.

Hendricks and Bolton both thought of themselves as good cops. They were, according to all of their evaluations. During their day and swing shifts, they were top performers on their crew. Even on mids, when they both slept three to four hours, they did as much as every other squad car detail. Their Officer Performance Reports (OPR) were outstanding, and both were in line for promotion at the next cycle. With their rotating schedule, Hendricks and Bolton were partnered about once a month for their six shifts of mids. They were careful about it, but they perfected their sleeping on the job routine. They felt no guilt about it; it was more like they were avoiding a toxic substance, that of not getting enough rest.

Everything was going well.

Being sound asleep doesn't protect your ears from the deafening crack of a high-caliber pistol fired at close range. Pamela felt like she'd been struck in the head with a shovel and the first thing her eyes could focus on was the windshield covered in blood and gore. She instinctively reached for her sidearm and opened the passenger door.

Hendricks was slumped in the driver's seat with his head resting on the steering wheel. She could see the hole in the back of his head but not the exit wound, probably through the forehead which was now facing down. She unholstered her gun as she exited the car. It took her a few seconds to determine that she was in upper Queen Anne as she could see across to the Space Needle.

There was no one on the street in any direction.

She looked at her watch: 04:39.

She called in the shooting as she desperately tried to make sense of the scene. She had a lot to explain, and very soon.

She noticed that the car wasn't running. Why had Hendricks parked at this location? What in the fuck had happened?

How much had Bolton missed between the gunshot and when she was able to focus? She was taking deep breaths as she walked down the street trying to catch a glimpse of someone or something fleeing the scene. Lights were going on in a couple of nearby homes.

The shooter must have been on foot, or possibly on a bicycle. She was certain she would have heard a vehicle.

She calculated that at the most, only five seconds could have passed before she was able to engage on the crime scene. That was more than enough time for someone to run away or ride away quietly on a bike. They were in the middle of a block and a car going in either direction would have taken longer than this to turn off down another street.

Well before the first response vehicle came speeding towards her, Officer Bolton realized she knew who'd murdered her new partner.

This was no great leap of deductive reasoning on her part. Cops always know who kills the wife, or boyfriend. Uxoricide was the term for a man killing his wife, although not a word any cop would use, nor would any social worker. What cops and social workers knew through experience was that when women were murdered, it's statistically the husband, lover, or piece-of-shit ex-husband who top the list of suspects.

Of all the things for Pamela to be thinking about in this moment, trying to come up with the word for when a husband murders his wife's lover wasn't a good use of her time, not now. She had a story to construct, one that didn't involve her being passed out in her patrol car. What percentage of men were killed by a jealous husband wasn't an easy statistic to glean as there were too many foggy areas for social scientists to calculate. There were variables like answering if the man killed was actually the woman's lover, or just suspected by the husband.

Most of these crimes of passion occur in the home, more than half. They call it domestic violence for a reason. Bolton's husband chose to make it happen while she was on duty, sitting in her patrol car next to her partner.

Why in the hell would he do that? Pamela couldn't get this thought out of her head even though she had bigger problems to face. She dug deep to keep from crying. She had time for that later, she thought. Instead of succumbing to her emotions, she thought about vengeance. She needed a clear head as soon as the first patrol car stopped and started asking her what happened at this gruesome scene.

That was going to happen in five, four, three, two...

How could a law enforcement professional like Bolton explain that she hadn't seen or heard anything when her partner was murdered as she sat next to him in their patrol car? Bolton was desperately trying to summon what she'd remembered up to that moment. How long had she been asleep? They were supposed to be driving, not parked on a quiet street and full of potential witnesses to a cop, perhaps two, passed out in a patrol car.

The real questions would come later. For the moment, this was a very active crime scene with a suspect on the loose, a suspect who'd just murdered an on-duty policeman. Bolton welcomed the chaos as not one but three more squad cars rolled up along with an ambulance. Citizens appeared on the street, moving in as two patrolmen motioned them to keep their distance as they taped off the crime scene. The pandemonium gave her time to formulate a story that would hold water.

She took this interval to look at her phone which would tell her exactly where they'd been and how long the car had been parked on this street. They'd driven up Counter-Balance Hill just over eighteen minutes before the shooting, turned left at the top of the hill and circled the neighborhood. This wasn't their sector for the evening, but that wasn't a problem. It had been a quiet night and they could have a million explanations for driving in this wealthy neighborhood with homes over one hundred years old. Bolton was asleep for all of it since they'd left the downtown area over thirty minutes prior to the shooting.

Why had Hendricks driven up to this area? Why did he park? Bolton had no idea and now this was all going to come out in an officer shooting investigation. She'd have no answers for the shooting board, but she knew what to say. She was a cop. She knew to say as little as possible. Saying nothing at all is the best strategy, but she didn't think that was going to fly, not with an official board.

For the moment, as far as what she said to the officers arriving at the scene, she told the truth. She didn't see a damn thing. No shooter, no fleeing vehicle, nothing. She didn't even hear anything after the gunshot blew her hearing to hell inside the car. From the splatter and the noise, Bolton thought that the shot was fired at close range, almost inside the window of the patrol car.

Cops were already knocking on doors near the scene. Bolton wasn't worried about witnesses, at least from the homes. Even if someone had been looking out the window at the precise moment of the shooting at a little after four-thirty in the morning, what could they report? She felt horrible that she was trying to cover her own ass about sleeping on the job, but that's about all she could worry about now. Even if she'd been wide awake, how could she have stopped someone from creeping up to the patrol car and firing a point-blank round into the back of her partner's head? She didn't plan to get fired in disgrace over it.

She barely knew him. And yet, she knew enough about him to know who had killed him.

It was no secret in the department that Bolton's soon-to-be ex-husband was a piece of work: a serial womanizer, violent by nature, and with a temper that had almost cost him his career on three occasions. He was her supervisor when she was just out of the academy and he pursued the beautiful new recruit mercilessly in violation of Seattle PD policy regarding fraternization between the ranks. Eight months after they met, they were married. It didn't take Pamela long to realize that she'd made a grievous error in judgment.

Terrance James Albright, or Sergeant Albright, went by TJ in the SPD. Of course, he had a nickname, most assholes had nicknames. TJ was an enormous asshole, but the young Pamela was impressed by his machismo, his stature on her crew, but mostly by his looks. He was like a billboard poster of a cop at an imperious 6'4" and built like a Seahawks defensive back.

It didn't take long after their wedding vows for TJ's slimier qualities to become frighteningly apparent. His unprovoked and insane jealousy came at Pamela out of nowhere, and although she was very young and just barely an adult, she had enough self-respect and confidence to walk away and not look back.

Pamela bailed out of the marriage after a bit over two years, now living on her own as she worked through the divorce procedures. Her ex wasn't taking it well, something she thought was odd as she caught him cheating on her, caught as in *en flagrante delicto*, as in fucking some whore—literally, a prostitute—in their own bed, her bed. The only upside to that sad story was that Pamela had dozens of reasons for leaving him before that image was burned into her head.

A supervisor was at the scene of the shooting forty-three minutes after Officer Bolton called it in. This had given her more than enough time to pull herself together and think clearly. She'd never been involved in any sort of shooting before, and this was the first time a cop had been shot in fourteen years at SPD. It would be a circus in the department, and even more so in the media. She had no idea what to expect. She felt that having a union lawyer present during her debriefing would be a good idea.

All that she knew for certain was that she couldn't admit that she'd been fast asleep for probably a half an hour before her partner was gunned down on a city street.

She was treated deferentially during the first round of questions, although her supervisor was having a difficult time understanding how she hadn't seen anything. Her story was that the deafening crack of the gunshot, and the blood on the windshield had prevented her from making an ID on the shooter, and it had taken her a couple of seconds to recover and get out of the car. This would've been more than enough time for the shooter to escape on foot.

They had been parked on West Prospect Street facing east, just below Kerry Park. Bolton said that she thought the shooter could have run down the grassy hill just below the passenger side of the patrol car. By the time Bolton exited the vehicle, the shooter could have already been at the bottom of the steep hill, but Bolton had looked east and west down the street expecting to see a fleeing vehicle, not immediately expecting someone on foot.

She was given a urinalysis and a blood test for alcohol, neither of which were a problem. When she was finally released, her supervisor gave her his condolences on the loss of her partner and told her there was nothing for her to worry about.

"Go home, try to get some sleep, but we'll need you back here later this afternoon."

Bolton knew better than to think this was over.

The next round of questioning seemed more like an interrogation. Boltons wondered why she wasn't cuffed to the table like a suspect. This time it was the shooting board made up of senior department officials and a public prosecutor.

"Officer Bolton, were you asleep on the job when the shooting took place?"

Bolton thought she took the question rather well as she'd anticipated this, at least in her worst-case scenario version. It was an easy question to answer, and she had a good idea why it was asked.

Because all cops have slept on the job during mids.

Hendricks answered not only in the negative, but in the military version.

"Fuck no, sir!"

The board didn't press this because they had nothing to go on and were fishing.

Slightly less than two hours later, it was over.

Bolton walked out into the hallway where she was met by Sergeant TJ Albright, in full dress uniform. Albright stepped directly in front of Pamela, blocking her forward progress.

"Sorry to hear about your partner."

"You need to listen to this, you fucking pig. Don't ever come this close to me again. If you do, I'll kill you, I swear," she said without a trace of nervousness. "I know it was you, cocksucker."

Albright didn't answer.

"You don't like it when I fuck other guys? Get used to it because I'm going to fuck every man in this department, all of them except you."

During the hearing, Bolton told the shooting board about her pending divorce, her husband's jealousy, and her suspicion that TJ Albright may have been involved. That's how much Pamela hated her husband. When she discovered that he had an airtight alibi the morning Hendricks was murdered, she was even more certain of his guilt. Who would have an alibi at 04:30? He had someone else do it, but he was responsible.

SPD had immediately investigated after Bolton's disclosure. Albright had been at his father's home in Spanyallup, at least a forty-five-minute drive from Seattle. He was cleared as a suspect, but Hendricks knew there was more to it.

Albright's brother also lived in the completely charmless sprawl of Spanyallup where the brothers were born. The guy made Pamela's skin crawl from the first time she met him and went way out of her way not to have anything to do with him during her short and unhappy marriage to his brother. The brother, Thaddeus, or Tad Albright was a real piece of shit. Divorced three times, with five kids: two from the first, two from the second, and one from the last. A deadbeat dad arrested three times on domestic violence charges, and currently unemployed. Albright's father had also been arrested for abuse, although never convicted as the wife—now deceased—had dropped the charges against her husband on three separate occasions.

This is what sociologists would call a pattern of violence, something Bolton learned after her own domestic abuse experience began only months after her wedding day. Her first thought after TJ accused her of flirting with other officers at work and threatening to harm her was that she did a piss-poor job of vetting her new husband. Had she known that his father and brother were both serial abusers, it would've dampened her infatuation for their son and brother. The writing was on the wall, had she bothered to read it.

Bolton never reported her husband for abuse fearing that it would've labeled her as a victim, which wouldn't have boded well for her career, or so she thought. This meant that there was absolutely no record that Sergeant Terrence James Albright was anything less than a perfect husband. Even had she reported Albright's often violent behavior, it was hardly proof that he was responsible for the murder of a fellow police officer. No one could even prove that she and Hendricks were having an affair.

Bolton didn't have the faintest hope of her husband being arrested for Hendrick's death, but she wanted to make him pay, to make all of them pay.

It was immediately obvious to her that all three of the Albright men were involved in the slaying. While the father claimed he was with TJ all evening, the younger brother had less of a bullet-proof alibi, not that he really needed one as he was a few steps away from the situation.

***

"So, why did it take you so long to leave him?" Hendricks had asked Pamela during one of their long conversations during a shift.

"I think it's because I'm so adverse to change, probably why I'll just stay at this job the rest of my life instead of exploring some other option."

She only had one goal to achieve in her law enforcement career, at least for now. She wanted to drive Sergeant Albright over the deep end, to provoke him to a point where he'd snap. She knew her husband had murdered her new partner, probably using his half-witted younger brother to carry out the crime. She also knew just enough about the law to understand that the brothers were going to get away with the murder.

Bolton had spoken with the lead homicide investigator on the case, and Detective Samuels admitted that he had less than nothing as far as a lead. There was no gun, no shell casing, no witnesses, and no motive other than murdering a cop. Every cop who'd ever made an arrest had enemies, but there was no one Hendricks had put away that threw up any red flags in the investigation.

What Terrance James Albright could prove was that he'd been drinking in a bar in Spanyallup, about sixty miles south of Seattle, with his father, his brother, and several friends until two o'clock in the morning. After closing, he and his father had taken a taxi to his father's house, also in Spanyallup, arriving at somewhere around 03:40 making it impossible for him to have been in Seattle less than an hour later when the shooting took place.

Detective Samuels felt he didn't even have cause to bring in Albright's brother for questioning, but he made a courtesy call to his trailer in Spanyallup. He wasn't at leisure to discuss the conversation with Bolton, but Samuels let her know that short of Tad Albright confessing to the murder, as far as the investigation was concerned, he wasn't a suspect. They had no suspects or persons of interest in the shooting death of Seattle Police Officer Dale Hendricks.

And that is how you get away with murder. The first rule is that you never kill anyone with whom you have any sort of connection. Bolton knew that why serial killers are so difficult to stop was they have no intersection with the people they murder—other than the crime itself. If they aren't caught at the scene, tracking them down is an enormous challenge.

***

The thing about being a cop is that you got to know an extraordinary number of complete scumbags, something that was simply part of the job, a big part of the job. You made enemies of most of the filth at the bottom of the barrel of humanity, but you were also obliged to forge alliances with criminals to obtain leverage against even worse people. You needed to maintain a host of relationships with a range of offenders from thieves, drug dealers, and sometimes even murderers, or at least individuals suspected of it. Whether it was cooperation or conspiracy, you did them favors and they did you favors.

Bolton needed a favor, and she knew exactly who to call on.

Pamela met Abdul Malik on her third month out of the academy. Abdul was a Muslim convert by way of the Corcoran state prison in California where he spent four years for armed robbery. Abdul worked, at least ostensibly, at his mother's fried chicken restaurant and take-out joint in the SoDo district, short for South of the Dome even though the old stadium had been dynamited years ago. The restaurant was popular and a favorite with cops.

It was suspected that Abdul used the restaurant to launder money he made in marijuana and cocaine sales. However, he'd never been arrested for the suspected money laundering or drug sales. Abdul was no major player in the local drug world, and he kept an extremely low profile. Cops liked his mother and her fried chicken. Bolton's only complaint was that the joint was too far from her apartment in Freemont for her to eat there as much as she would've liked.

She went there quite a lot while on patrol, but she liked the place and the atmosphere and hung out there on her own time, once she moved out on her husband. She enjoyed her conversations with the ex-felon. Abdul and Bolton were the same age, as they discovered after a few meetings at the restaurant. They also were big baseball fans and life-long Mariners groupies.

Bolton wouldn't exactly consider that the two were friends, but it had definitely evolved to the "I'll do you a favor and you can do me a favor" stage in their relationship.

Bolton wasn't looking for the usual cop-perp sort of favor when she gave Abdul Malik a bundle of cocaine she'd come across in a deal while on patrol with her former training officer Patrick Markham, a useless lump of shit like none other in the department. The two cops had been patrolling late at night through the parking lot of one of the more notorious motels on Aurora Avenue where Markham liked trolling for prostitutes he could flirt with.

Bolton was driving through a steady Seattle rain when she saw two men standing near a parked vehicle. She slammed on the brakes, put the patrol car in park, and ran towards them, trying to induce a response from the suspicious pair.

The two fled in opposite directions, one of them with a shoebox-sized package under his arm. Bolton went after the package. Officer Markham decided to keep his seat in the heated and dry patrol car. She chased the runner around the back of the motel though a no-man's-land of abandoned appliances and tangled chain link fences. She was gaining on him when the perpetrator dropped the package.

143

Bolton stopped and recovered it, allowing the man to escape. It wasn't a split-second decision when she decided to ditch the package in a secure place and come back for it later. She'd fantasized about how she'd pull off a score since before she even became a cop. Most cops had probably done the same, at least thought about it. Bolton quickly decided that this situation was perfect, what in the military was called a target of opportunity. It was too good to pass up.

Her partner was a worthless hump who wouldn't be a problem, always choosing the path of least resistance and the minimum of effort. When she returned to the squad car, she told Markham that the kid had cans of spray paint, and she assumed they were writing graffiti at the motel.

"Thank God I didn't bother to chase two little shits with cans of paint. You about gave me a heart attack," Markham told her.

Hendricks would have much preferred a bundle of cash, but it turned out to be over two kilograms of cocaine when she finally recovered the package three days later. What the hell was she going to do with cocaine?

In a very complicated and delicate arrangement, she gave the package to Abdul Malik. Abdul had been the one who gave Bolton the tip about a possible drug buy, at a very specific time, at a very specific ratty motel on Aurora Avenue. Bolton hadn't asked for details and figured it was a rival or someone who'd rubbed Abdul the wrong way at some point.

She didn't want any money for the exchange—Bolton didn't feel that she was quite at that level of corruption so early in her career—but it was understood that she'd done Abdul a considerable favor. Bolton left it at that, with anything that might transpire between them in the future left unsaid. In fact, nothing was ever said about it between the two.

But now Pamela was about to collect on her favor.

Bolton had asked quite a lot, but two kilograms of decent cocaine goes a long way. In this case, it meant that Tad Albright was found dead in his squalid trailer by a guy selling magazine subscriptions door-to-door. He said the door was cracked open and he could plainly see Tad Albright hanging from a leather strap attached to a closet door. The cause of death was determined to be auto-erotica asphyxiation, which, although not exactly an epidemic like methamphetamines, wasn't the first time it had occurred in Spanyallup.

In a perfect world, Bolton would've had Tad jerking off to child pornography, but she didn't even want to attempt to find anything so vile, even when it would be used to slander a cop killing piece-of-shit. Instead, Tad's computer was filled with gay fatty porn, a genre she hadn't known was even a thing.

"To each his own."

That was exactly what Bolton said to TJ Albright at the station when they ran into each other, a run-in planned by Bolton a week after TJ's brother died.

"Gay fatty porn. They call it chubby gay," she said. "What will they think of next, right?"

Albright didn't even look up and tried to move by Bolton in the narrow hallway.

"Man, that magazine salesman's social media account really went viral. A total asshole thing to do, right?"

The magazine salesman was also part of Bolton's conspiracy, orchestrated brilliantly by Abdul Malik and his associates. The viral video guy was an actual local salesman who was bribed to go to the trailer and photo bomb the internet with Tad Albright's secret shame.

Quality photos of Tad Albright's death scene were posted on an anonymous social media account—something impossible to undo.

Both officers were in uniform in the hallway of the precinct. Even so, Bolton was expecting Albright to attack her, to assault her in some manner. The fact that he didn't either proved he had a modicum of control, or the more likely answer, that he was stunned by his brother's "suicide."

Pamela couldn't discern if Albright was even remotely suspicious that his brother's death may not have been an accident. After their brief time together, Bolton had come to the conclusion that TJ Albright wasn't at all clever, but this level of stupidity almost made her want to tell him that his brother's death was no accident.

"Ever jerk off with a belt around your neck?"

"Get the fuck away from me."

"Don't be so closed-minded. You're telling me you've never done it?"

Albright tried to push past his tormenter, but Bolton planted herself squarely in front of the giant.

"There's a really fine line between extasy and unconsciousness, and then it's all over. Then you shit yourself, as in the case of young Tad," Pamela said. "At least he had his pants off, or down, but still. What. A. Mess!"

Albright said nothing.

"I guess at that point your worries are over, right?"

"I'm going to fucking kill you, bitch."

"OK, but you really need to talk about these anger issues, or the stress just builds up."

Albright finally made it by Bolton who couldn't resist one final shot.

"Pretty amazing the quality of video on cell phones these days, huh? You could see the video on his computer screen, bunch of fat guys plowing each other daisy-chain style."

Bolton and Abdul were in front of the baseball stadium buying polish hot dogs from her favorite cart. The crowd on a Tuesday night for the second-to-last place team was abysmal.

"Dude, I never, and I mean never-fucking-ever want to get on your shit list. You're like some sort of mad genius for raining down hate on someone," Abdul said.

"You're being too modest about your contribution."

"I was just the carpenter; you were the architect. Hell, I wasn't even that. I was just the foreman."

Bolton ate her dog. Abdul Malik saved his bag of sunflower seeds for the first pitch. It was their first baseball game together.

"You're not worried about big brother coming after you?" Abdul asked.

"I'm not worried about it; I'm absolutely counting on it. I'm practically begging him."

She relayed the exchange in the hallway she'd had with Albright.

"Damn, man. You're fucking evil."

"Me? No."

"And he didn't do anything?"

"I was as incredulous as you are now,' Bolton said as they walked into the stadium.

Abdul Malik kept score, she didn't. Both enjoyed baseball almost as much as drinking beer. Pamela was more of a baseball historian, the color commentator, while Abdul was the statistician.

By the bottom of the ninth, with the home team losing 0-5, they had their section completely to themselves.

"So, what's your next move against this murderous piece-of-shit?" Abdul asked.

"I want him to suffer. What I really want is for him to land in prison. There's no way he'll go down for killing Hendricks, but anything will do. Hard time for a cop is as hard as it gets. I'm thinking on it."

"My advice to you: think fucking faster because he'll come after you."

A ground out to the infield ended the game for the hapless pride of Seattle. The two fans shook hands and walked in opposite directions on First Avenue. Bolton unlocked her bike where she'd left it at the bar where the two met before the game, the same bar she'd always had her first drink before a game. Baseball is nothing but tradition, and it has countless traditions.

Riding her bicycle home slightly drunk after a game seemed to have become another tradition for Bolton. She cursed this tradition while humping up the two hills between the stadium and her over-priced and super-small apartment in Fremont. She arrived at her building and began to lock her bike to the stair railing when she heard footsteps behind her. She turned to find TJ Albright and his father, her father-in-law walking towards her. Albright held his hands up, palms facing Hendricks.

"Just here to talk," he said. "How about we go inside?"

"How about we do this out in the open? Let's take a walk," she said. "Both of you in front of me and keep your hands where I can see them."

They walked towards the street and Bolton told them to turn right and walk down Freemont Avenue.

"So, talk," she ordered.

"You can only push me so far, Pam. Just back off, like all the way, and we'll have no problems."

"Or what?"

"What do you think, bitch?"

"Spell it out for me," she said, pushing aside the insult.

She wanted him to make a direct threat, more than anything it was just to see if he had the guts to do it.

"Or I'll kill you. How's that? Clear enough for you?"

"Listen, Terrence," she began, knowing that he hated his given name. "You got away with killing my partner. Bravo. But you think you'll get away with shooting me? I thought you were trying to get into robbery-homicide? You should know better."

Albright had nothing to say.

"Angry with me because he gave me the best orgasms of my life? I didn't have much to compare him with, you being a piece-of-fucking-shit, completely incapable-of-pleasing-a-woman kind of guy."

This was Pamela's first mention that Hendricks was her lover.

Albright was on the verge of violence; Bolton could sense it.

"We're not here to kill you, just give you a warning to back the fuck off," Albright said.

He was losing his cool and desperately trying not to show it.

"But I really like fucking with you, both of you."

She eyed the patriarch of the family. The father was only fifty-eight but looked twenty years older. He was like an older version of the meth-heads cops dealt with every night.

"Sorry about your son. A tragic loss, but take solace in knowing that he died doing what he loved to do…"

The father was already on the verge of apoplexy.

"…jerking off with a belt around his neck, watching obese homos plow each other in the asshole."

Bolton made a very ceremonious sign of the cross.

"You just can't put a price tag on that," she said.

Of course, she could put a price on that, which was the going rate for almost two kilos of decent cocaine. Then, without meaning to, she burst out laughing.

"You fucking cunt!" the father screamed. "I'll kill you right here."

The old man swung a haymaker with his right arm, but Bolton backed up a step, then slapped his face so hard the old man spun completely around, falling down hard on the sidewalk, face-first.

"Don't make me hurt him," she warned her ex-lover.

Albright helped his father up on his feet.

"You both came armed to tell me to back off, and with death threats? Now I'm telling you that if I ever hear that you're mistreating a woman, I don't give a fuck if it's thirty years from now, you're going to hear from me, just like little Tad."

Bolton turned to walk back to her house but swung back around sharply.

"And tell your wife-beating father to crawl back to the cesspool where he lives and stay there."

Bolton knew that she could only push Albright so far before he'd feel absolutely compelled to strike out at her. Coming to her house had been a stupid move, but it didn't give Bolton any advantage unless she reported it. She wasn't looking for protection against Albright while at the same time she knew that this was far from over. There was only one way for it to be over, and both of them knew it.

The monstrously embarrassing death of his brother was almost payback for killing her lover, Bolton thought, but not quite. Christ, she thought, she liked Hendricks, and the sex was great, but it was just a fling. They just hooked up a bunch of times and drove together on mids. The biggest outrage was that her scummy husband killed him for something that meant little to either her or Hendricks. However, even though she and Hendricks were just friends with benefits, nothing more, she doubted that she'd be any angrier with her ex-husband had she been madly in love with Hendricks.

***

It really wasn't Bolton's thing, but Abdul loved sitting on the water. He said that looking out over the sea was the exact opposite of sitting inside a prison cell. They were drinking beer and eating fried squid at a tourist joint on the downtown waterfront. Bolton had explained the ultimatum given to Albright and the consequences she planned if the offer was rejected.

"I was never very clear on your relationship to Hendricks. You told me that you talked a lot of shit to your ex, but were you two lovers?" Abdul asked.

"No, man."

"See, I don't get that. You're taking this personally, to the extreme, like putting your life on the line, and you weren't really into him? Makes no damn sense."

"We were partners."

After a brief silence.

"And I hate scum like my ex who hurt women."

"I'm with you on that one, sister. I'm a mama's boy through and through, ask anyone at Corcoran. My mama came once a month."

"I swear, if find out this scumbag has a new girlfriend that he's slapping around, I'll walk up to him in the precinct and beat him to death with a brick."

"Wo, slow down, killer. You know better. Shit, you taught me. You could write the book on it, 'How to Get Away with Murder.' It'd be a bestseller for sure."

Abdul took a swig off his beer before continuing.

"Separation, like several degrees. Like doing the fuck-face brother the night of your birthday party at the pub with forty cops as your alibi. Shit, our alibi—that was a good party. Pure brilliance, Bolton."

Abdul sat back in his chair to reflect.

"I'm a criminal. Been one all my life, since I was twelve growing up in L.A. But you're a fucking master criminal."

He raised his glass, which Bolton tapped very reluctantly.

"When I'm motivated like I am, I feel inspiration," she admitted.

This had to be the strangest conversation to have ever occurred in the touristy seafood joint, where on this evening Bolton and Abdul Malik were probably the only two customers who lived in Seattle.

"OK, so you already know that this hick from Spanyallup isn't going to go for it, right?"

"I'm truly hoping he will. That's the god's truth."

"Shut the fuck up!" Abdul shouted in the very loud and crowded restaurant. "You don't believe in God, you only've told me a million times."

"I don't need God; I have a Plan B."

"I'd've been completely dumbfounded if you didn't," the former and current felon said.

Abdul raised his glass again.

"My next question is if I'm somehow a part of Plan B?"

"This is on me tonight, my friend," was Bolton's answer.

"I'd say 'fuck you' but the more you tell me about this guy, the less I like him."

Abdul stared Bolton down.

"I know that you don't come cheap. I'm working on that," Pamela said.

"I'd rather you think long and hard on the plan so no one goes to jail. That worries me more than how you'll pay for it."

"No one's going down but this guy."

"Very convincing, but remember that this guy, a police sergeant, is also gunning for your ass."

She hadn't forgotten. She knew the clock was ticking.

Bolton was alone on her days and swings, but on the graveyard shifts, she was assigned new partners, usually rookies.

Would Albright try the same move? A gunman walking up to the patrol car at a stop? Needless to say, the nights of Bolton taking a nap on the job were behind her.

The irony was that she felt a lot more vulnerable in her sleep-deprived state during her night shifts than she ever did when she slept on the job. On her last cycle of mids, Bolton actually had walking blackouts, blocks of time in which she couldn't recall anything when she tried to conjure them up the next day. Even when her partner described the redacted parts of the evening, it didn't register with her.

The graveyard shift would kill her before Albright got the chance.

She could barely ride her bike home after her second-to-last mid of the cycle and staggered up the stairs to her apartment. She'd had two beers with her partner after the shift which only made her feel even less human after five days of working nights. She threw her bag with her uniform on the floor and dropped down on her bed in civilian clothes, not even bothering to remove her shoes. It was ten-thirty in the morning, an ungodly hour to sleep.

Bolton woke up in a fog less than an hour later upon hearing something. She wasn't in such a stupor that she didn't reach for her service weapon on the bedside table. She always slept with a long pillow that she used to raise her leg, a technique to combat chronic back problems. She got out of bed and pulled the comforter over the pillow. It looked a lot like a body.

At first, she wasn't certain, but there was definitely someone in the apartment. She put herself in a corner facing the door to the bedroom. The door, which wasn't completely closed, began to open slowly. A man entered the bedroom wearing a mask. Bolton saw that he was too short to be Albright. The masked assailant fired four rounds into the pillow. Bolton fired a round into the ankle of her would-be assassin.

Albright's hired killer was just too pathetic to kill, a split-second decision she made even in her sleep-deprived state. She stood up from her crouch, walked over to the fallen hitman, and stomped on his wrist still holding the pistol. A broken wrist and a shattered ankle were two very painful injuries.

Bolton's first call was to the Seattle Police Department reporting the crime. Next, she called Sergeant TJ Albright who was on duty.

"You missed, asshole."

"Who's this?"

"Jesus, I know you're a complete fucking idiot, but even you can recognize a voice, especially of your ex."

Albright didn't respond.

"How long do you think it'll take for this complete loser to give you up? Even if you distanced yourself from your hired killer, it'll get back to you."

Albright mumbled something incoherent.

"I think I shot his fucking foot off, then crushed his wrist. He's in lock up, or he will be when the hospital's done with him. Did you pay him enough to keep quiet after that?"

Albright hung up. One of the first intelligent things he'd done so far.

Bolton knew that she shouldn't have communicated with Albright, especially by phone, but she couldn't pass up the chance to get inside his head. Besides, the phone she used was untraceable, and Albright had nothing to gain by reporting it.

She also knew that she was lucky that she heard the intruder in time, she had the graveyard shift to thank for that. She never slept soundly during the day; the slightest noise was enough to rock her out of a fitful sleep.

In the ensuing investigation that day, Bolton said she had no idea who would want to do her harm and made no mention of her soon-to-be ex-husband. She was confident that even if she accused Albright, there would be nothing to link him to this attempted murder of a Seattle police officer. If the assailant kept his mouth shut, Albright wouldn't have anything to worry about. Bolton wanted him to feel confident. She had plans.

There was no blowback with the investigation into Tad Albright's death as it had been determined to be accidental. There'd been no signs of a struggle, no evidence of other injuries that would suggest that he hadn't died during a solitary sex act gone wrong. Bolton had alibis that included many Seattle police officers.

In this assassination attempt, she was confident Albright had covered his tracks with the kind the precision expected of a cop who wanted to move up into robbery-homicide.

However, a promotion probably wasn't in Sergeant Albright's future, not if Bolton had any say in the matter.

The assailant was only too willing to cooperate and admitted that he'd been contracted by someone he couldn't identify to murder

Bolton—claiming he didn't know she was a cop—in exchange for a promise of releasing him on his drug charges that could have put him away for a decade. Nothing pointed to Albright, and even if a link had been made, this statement from a convicted drug dealer who'd attempted to murder a police officer wouldn't be overly prejudicial against Sergeant Albright, whose standing in the department, although not exemplary, was solid.

Bolton still had a card or two up her sleeve, some moves to make.

In their all-night-long conversations in the squad car, Pamela Bolton had told Hendricks that her husband, among all of his other faults, was a notorious womanizer. She suspected that he'd been cheating on her almost since they were first married. He frequented strip clubs, flirted with anything in a skirt, and seemed inordinately concerned with prostitution in his police patrols. He never tried to hide his online activity which included an exhaustive amount of porn streaming and dating websites. She found a dating application on his phone which he'd used to contact at least a half dozen women. Even after she caught him in the act in their own bed, Albright didn't bother hiding his username and password for the dating sites.

"He's such a typical police pig, no offense," Abdul Malik said to Bolton on another of their days at the ballpark.

"None taken. The truth is I don't really like cops."

"He likes blondes with big tits. What a surprise! I made this profile on the dating application," Abdul said, showing Bolton a picture on his phone.

"Damn, she a friend of yours?"

"Naw, man. Some minor porn star I'm hoping he's never seen before."

"I doubt that's possible."

Bolton took another look at the bimbo.

"Think he'll go for her?" Bolton asked.

"Dude, every guy on this site is dying to hook up with our girl. He'll take the bait, sooner or later. Sooner's my guess."

Sooner was two days later. Albright must have felt that he'd won the lottery when the fictitious Angel with the huge boobs agreed to meet him for a coffee or "maybe more" as she intimated.

"You almost have to admire a guy who recently murdered his ex-wife's partner, lost his brother in a tragic masturbation accident, and must be a suspect and under investigation in the attempted murder of his ex-wife, yet he doesn't take the eye off the ball of his true vocation: being a fucking scumbag," Abdul said.

"Reading his messages to this made-up whore is sickening," Bolton said.

Before she moved out on him, Bolton had one of her techie friends clone his phone and computer allowing her to see everything that he did on his phone and online.

"Maybe he's in love. Never understood the huge cartoon boobs," Abdul said. "To each his own."

"You mean, to each his fetish, his obsession. Yours is Asian women, so don't try to sound so superior," Bolton said.

"What's yours, Pamela?"

She needed a minute to consider this.

"At the moment, mine is my dead partner," he said. "So, when's the first date?"

The date was the following Monday, the slowest night of the week in Seattle. Albright arranged to meet his future wife in front of the Seattle Art Museum on First Avenue at ten o'clock in the evening. There was a late-night exhibition.

"This was his idea, probably trying to make it romantic, like that moron has ever been inside a museum in his life," Bolton said the night before the date.

"It's too open, too public. We need a more secluded place," Abdul said.

"If it looks dicey, we wait, find another window."

Abdul Malik had been modest, Hendricks thought. He was an excellent criminal.

The closest Albright had ever come to the Seattle Art Museum was the strip club that was a few doors down the street. He'd parked several blocks away to avoid paying and walked down First Avenue where he was spotted by Abdul who messaged the others involved in the caper.

Angel, or whatever her real name was, stood across the street from the museum. She held the handrail that led down the wide steps to Post Alley. She wasn't the porn star from the dating application, but her platinum blonde wig and stuffed brassiere made her into a reasonable facsimile.

Abdul Malik had no contact with Angel nor with her accomplice. They'd dealt through intermediaries, and the intermediaries worked through others. It was a simple operation with little chance for blow-back on Abdul, and even less on Bolton.

Albright saw the well-endowed blonde woman standing near the stairs.

Abdul had explained very clearly how this was to go down. If anything went haywire, the operation was scratched. It all depended on there being very few people in the street—the fewer the better. Abdul would be watching. If anything looked less than kosher, he'd blow a whistle calling it off.

There was no whistle. There was no one on the street.

Albright approached the hooker of his dreams. She was looking out to the sound, down the stairs.

"Angel," he called out to her when he was a few steps away.

She turned slowly.

Albright touched her shoulder as she turned.

"You look different," he said.

"Let's take a picture together of our first meeting," she said. "I love pictures."

Albright held out his camera. Angel took it from him with a giggle.

"Guys can't take good pictures. Let me do it."

She extended her arm to take the photograph.

"Wait. I want the statue of the guy with the hammer in the pic," Angel said as she spun them around with their backs to the museum, looking down over the stairs from the top step.

Angel held the camera out at arm's length. Albright put his arm on Angel's back and smiled. She graciously moved his arm down and rested his hand on the front side of her ample butt.

A man jogging down the street pushed Albright violently on his lower back, then raced down First Avenue.

Albright didn't just fall down the stairs, he was launched. He landed with a sickening thud six or seven steps below. At least at street level, no one had witnessed the accident, but there were hundreds of apartments looking down on the iconic stairs.

Angel walked smoothly away from her first and last date with the cop, heading up First Avenue towards the market. A sedan came to a stop. She got in, and as they drove away she took off her blonde wig, putting it in her handbag along with Albright's phone. The jogger had was long gone.

Albright was pronounced dead at the scene. No witnesses emerged and oil was found on his right shoe where Angel had steered him into a small pool of grease at the top of the stairs while they were posing for their photo.

Bolton was on duty on the other side of the city.

Investigators had nothing to go on and were compelled to deem it an accident. Bolton wasn't even questioned about the death.

When Abdul Malik and Bolton dared to meet again a full three weeks later, they met at a pub in Ballard, neural ground for both of them and an unlikely place for anyone to recognize either of them. There was a sparse Tuesday night crowd, and they chose a booth against the back wall.

"I was almost at the point of not giving a shit if I had to go down for this guy, but your people pulled it off like a Mossad operation," Bolton said.

"It was all you, your plan all the way," Abdul answered. "But, hell yeah. It went down like clockwork. I saw the whole thing, start to finish. Wish I'd filmed it."

"How'd the gal do?"

"She was a star. Like you said, Mossad ain't got nothing on her," Abdul said. "That was brilliant how you got him to hand over his phone."

Bolton had thought it all through from start to finish, anticipating a thousand different permutations of the plan, of what could happen and how to follow up with a counter.

"I'm still worried about the father," Bolton said.

"Damn, girl. You gonna take out the whole family? Who's next? Cousins? Uncles? His kindergarten teacher?"

"I just don't want to be looking over my back until that old creep drops dead from a heart attack or whatever."

"Leave me out of this one. I'd suggest you leave it alone, too. Three in one family? That's just begging to get busted."

She knew that Abdul Malik was one hundred percent correct on that point.

"You need to realize that you're, like, legitimately good at this criminal bullshit. Right?"

Bolton took a healthy swig from her pint of ale instead of answering.

"You need to be making money at it. We need to be making money at it."

"You got paid for all this," Pamela reminded her friend.

"I'm not complaining but look how easy it was for you to take down those bitches at the motel."

"If I've learned one thing as a cop, it's that you're an idiot to press your luck. Crooks always go down, sooner or later. If I had you in my sights, you'd be serving time again."

"I wish I could argue with you on that. Good news is that we're friends. Shit, more than that. We're partners," Abdul said.

"We're friends whose criminal interests intersect from time to time," Bolton corrected Abdul.

"Now you're talking like my lawyer."

"You need a lawyer who's a lot smarter than I, Abdul. I pray I never need one."

Abdul raised his glass to toast to not needing lawyers.

"I still can't believe that you did all this, and you weren't even sleeping with the guy."

Bolton didn't respond.

Abdul Malik immediately understood the silence.

"Motherfucker. I knew it. Of course, you two were lovers. You had me fooled, but that's the only way this makes any sense."

Bolton's friend needed time to take in this new revelation.

"I guess it's pretty romantic, if you think about it."

"The less I think about it the better," she answered. "I just hope it's finished."

"Why wouldn't it be? You can't be worried about the father. Dude is like half-dead already."

"I was still married to that fucking creep, so daddy and I are related. I wouldn't put it past him to try to get dealt in on Terrence's insurance I'll be collecting."

Abdul was shocked for the second time that evening.

"You telling me you're getting paid, too?" he asked. "You never mentioned that."

"We aren't officially divorced yet. I get his insurance."

Abdul sat back in his chair to consider this.

"You are seriously a criminal mastermind."

"The less I talk about any of this, the better off we'll both be," Bolton said. "That's like rule number one in crime, but I don't have to tell you that."

Another round of beers came to the table.

Pamela raised her new glass.

"Here's to never talking about this again," she proposed.

They toasted.

"All I'm saying, Pamela, is that you're on the wrong side of the law, at least from a financial perspective."

A WINDOW OPENS

The place had swinging doors. No joke. I guess nobody told them to stop making bars this way in Chihuahua. Didn't bother paving the street either, just dust and gravel. Prices were above the bar, hand-written in chalk. The cost for a shot of tequila, like everything else in the bar, probably hadn't changed much in a hundred years. I got a *Tecate* and tried to disappear at a table in a back corner.

The jukebox, loaded with old-school rancheras, was at full volume, Vicente Fernández belting out *Volver, Volver*. I had no problem with the music, and if the beer were any colder, it'd be ice. It all would've been fine except I was terrified.

The place was called the Star of Chihuahua, which made me chuckle. As a kid, I'd draw a star with lines intersecting at a center point, which also looked like an asshole, so I guess the name fit. When you get a summons from the cartel, your options are limited; they choose the location. I chose to follow orders, often the best way to stay alive, except when it isn't. Dealing arms to narcos was a high-risk enterprise, even when they were happy. They weren't.

Touchy bastards even when things were going well. Customs seized a shipment of M4 carbines which set off fireworks in the cartel. To me, this was nothing more than a slight hiccup, the price of doing business. I told them I could get another shipment together in a week; promised to escort this one through personally. They were losing their minds even though they already had enough firepower to take on the Texas National Guard.

They assumed I'd sold the guns to the Juárez people, that I was arming their enemies, playing both sides. I admired that they came right out with the accusation, then threatened to kill me—I hate passive-aggressive types. Lately, cartel killings were more than double automobile fatalities in Mexico. I took their threat seriously.

Your first instinct is to run, but that didn't always go well for the runners. Sometimes they'd forget about you, other times they'd keep

165

looking until someone walks up to you in the line at a busy supermarket in Seattle two years later and shoots you dead. They were all about making a statement, like when the Soviets murdered Trotsky—wasn't just about killing him. I knew these people. I'd seen their "messages" hanging upside down from overpasses. Murder was a tool they used as casually as a carpenter his hammer. I was the nail in this scenario, but thought I could talk my way out.

I was hoping that the six AK47s I'd crossed the border with this morning would smooth things over, a goodwill gesture, if you can say that about assault rifles. I took a huge risk driving the guns across myself, but an even bigger gamble showing up in this dump to meet with Xavier, my only contact with the cartel. We got along, had even hung out a few times, but I knew what he'd do if push came to "put one in the gringo's dome." You didn't have friends in this business, not if you were smart and liked having birthdays.

Two hours, twenty-two classic ranchera ballads, and four beers later, Xavier was a no-show, weird because the guy usually texted me constantly before a meet up, like a giddy teen before a first date. I didn't know if I'd dodged a bullet or would step into an ambush on the way back to the van.

I went to the bar to settle up. On the TV, a news bulletin of a horrific shootout near Juárez. Dozens killed, drug related—of course—Sinaloa and Juárez gangs going at it. Happened hours earlier, police still sifting through the rubble.

Please include Xavier in that body count, I prayed. This could be one of those "when God closes a door, he opens a window" moments.

I swore earlier today that if I walked away, I'd give this up, but now I had six *cuernos* to sell. No shortage of buyers in Mexico, three right here in Chihuahua. The window should still be open after that. Right?

CRIME FAMILY

When you had the keys, it didn't even feel like stealing.

He called himself Blake, but lots of people, even school friends and teachers didn't know if that was his first or last name. He got by with only one. He felt his parents hadn't earned the right to give him a name, so he started to use just one of the two he was given. He'd make the change official when he was an adult, or maybe he'd give himself another name. The more he thought about that idea, the more reasonable it seemed for everyone to name themselves.

It was getting tricky in the age of high-tech to by-pass automobile ignition systems, to hotwire a car, at least a lot more difficult than it used to be, or so he was told by people who'd been doing it a while. A lot of the nihilistic punks were still doing the car-jacking thing, but that meant heavy jail time and ranked high on police tasking priorities, much higher than regular grand theft. Two sixteen-year-olds were shot dead recently jacking a car in the parking lot of a shopping mall in Boca Raton. Wasn't even the law that did it but the owner.

It was all about risk versus reward, something Blake learned almost from the start. First of all, you never even bothered unless it was something that was worth your time and trouble. Blake had a shopping list of models, always knew exactly what he was going to boost, and the payday that would come with it. Sure, it was a huge rush driving away in an expensive car that wasn't yours, but he wasn't doing it for thrills.

Another important consideration was exposure. You spent as little time as possible inside the vehicle, which meant having someone lined up to take it off your hands as soon as you were in the clear.

He'd been working with a group from Hialeah for several months. No problems. So far, so good, but he'd heard of a guy before him who had cops following after the withdrawal—that was this team's name for the heist, the withdrawal. The kid led the cops right to the drop point and they busted him and the two guys from the second team there to pick it up. The group wasn't too happy with that, to put it very mildly. The kid never made it out of county lock-up. Knifed, or so the story went.

Simple, you spend as little time in the item—another word of theirs for the car. You made absolutely sure you were in the clear, then you went to the drop area that was prearranged. You didn't bring anything with you. No personal cell phone, no identification, and no weapons, not even a knife. That was group policy. No armed resistance if you were facing arrest or being apprehended. If you got into a huff with the owner, that was on you to resolve, but no weapons. Running always worked for Blake. Most of the items he withdrew belonged to older, rich assholes, many of them women. He'd only had three occasions when he was interrupted and had to abandon the item and run like hell. One time the guy wasn't so old and not slow at all, and he was big as hell. Scared the living shit out of Blake, but the guy didn't have much interest in running down some teenager and gave up after a block.

So far, he'd never had a run-in with the cops, not ever. If he did get caught, he was hoping that being a minor would count for something in court, but you never knew these days and kids were tried as adults all the time, went to real prisons. It was usually driving to the drop off area when morons got busted, mostly for stupid shit like speeding, or making an illegal turn. His plan was that if he ever got made while driving from the boost to payday, he'd slam on the brakes and run like hell while leaving the car in drive, giving the cops one more headache to deal with.

He was smarter than most. He knew that you had to drive like an old man, or a kid in driver education class, like he was taking at school this semester. The teacher couldn't believe how well he drove. Blake had a lot of practice, this being his second year of withdrawing items, or grand theft auto as he called it—along with other video gamers. But that was before hooking up with this team. He knew others working this same scam who'd run the damn car into the ground just for fun. One kid wrapped a perfectly good item around a light post. He was lucky for a lot of things, like not ending up in the hospital from the accident, not getting busted, and not getting stomped for smashing up a great item.

Blake didn't really like the driving part. It was just a job to him and driving was no more exciting to him as was his driver's education class in high school. He didn't care about cars and never planned to have one. He hated traffic more than he felt any love for the expensive machines he was stealing; it didn't matter what you were driving, if you were stuck in a quagmire on I-95, and that described every day of the week, including Sundays, you were hating life. Cars were for suckers, at least in Blake's book. Most people couldn't afford their item and everyone knew that they were a terrible investment.

The thing was, he was really good at the whole withdrawal game. He was taking down three vehicles a week sometimes and making a small fortune on each item he dropped off, at least a small fortune for a high school kid. He got more for the truly exotic models, but he'd only been able to withdraw two so far in eight months. He got another extra cash bonus for the luxury SUVs if they were black. They loved the black SUVs, or someone did, somewhere.

He wouldn't say it was easy work. He had to spend quite a lot of time finding his items. He had to change his *modus operandi* every so often so as not to have a pattern that the law could use to leapfrog ahead of him. What set Blake apart from most of the others doing withdrawals was his originality, his creativity, his ability to think outside the box—to borrow a very tired expression but not usually associated with grand theft.

His first scam turned out to be a little too risky, although it yielded almost ten items before he abandoned the strategy. He'd scout neighborhoods for the items on his list. When he found what he was looking for, he returned to the homes and simply walked into the house and take the keys from a purse. Literally every modestly-priced home in the Miami area had some sort of home security system, but this only worked if the doors were closed. Blake would walk into the back yard and slide open a screen door. In most cases, the purse he was looking for was on a table near the front door. He'd remove the key, walk back through the back door, get in the item parked in the driveway, and be on his way.

After a couple of very close calls, he decided to retire this plan, or at least use it only when the perfect opportunity presented itself.

He had a friend who worked at one of the more upscale fitness centers in South Beach who would wave him through the entrance after he had spotted his quarry parking his item in the attached garage. He'd follow the guy into the changing room and then break open his locker—a lot easier to do than by-pass an ignition on a brand-new SUV. The poor slob wouldn't even know he'd been had until he was finished with his workout. Of course, this plan had a short shelf-life, so he used it sparingly. He found a couple of other gyms and ran the same ploy.

He had another idea to deflect heat away from the gym thefts. He was mostly after one make of SUV, which all had keys that looked exactly alike except for the machining. He obtained blank keys for the model and had them machined randomly. When he stole the key at the gyms, he replaced the stolen key with one of the dummies. They never knew that their keys had been stolen at the gym because they'd never know that the key on their ring wasn't for their vehicles.

Separating drivers from their keys, that was what became his obsession. It was odd because Blake had never shoplifted anything in his life. Thou shalt not steal were four words he really didn't have a big problem obeying. He just figured that the items he was withdrawing were from rich assholes, the victims in what he considered victimless crimes. They all had insurance. Hell, he figured half of them were probably thrilled not to have to make their monthly payments.

He worked valet parking spots at the top restaurants in Coconut Grove and South Beach. The valets worked in groups of at least two and it was just a matter of having them both away from their station at the same time. He'd use the lovely Greta Eriksen in these scams, Greta was a senior at Fort Lauderdale High School and one of the hottest women Blake had ever seen. Seventeen years old and looked twenty-five. She lived with her sort of lower-middle class mother but her father had money, the CEO of some fast-food franchise, and Greta carried herself like she had everything.

Greta had passed through all the usual pathologies of a kid from a broken home and parents who didn't give a shit. She had a lot in common with Blake, minus the rich dad bit in his case. She loved being a criminal more than her other self-destructive habits like drugs or sex. Unfortunately for Blake, they were "just friends," but he was an optimist. They didn't work together much, but when they did, it was like art, like those people who win dance contests. He paid her way too much for her services, but he was thinking more long-term, she would always be useful down the line.

For the valet scams, she'd pull up in one of her dad's cars that she stole for the night—her mom drove a Honda. She flirted with the valet when she dropped off her car while Blake kept an eye on what keys were going where from a discreet distance. She had one earphone plugged in and he'd tell her which number they needed. She could either get what they needed on the way in, or the way out thirty minutes later while the car owners were having a long dinner inside.

He watched as she flirted and didn't know whether to envy or pity the poor bastards as she worked a game on them. She probably could have talked them into stealing the car themselves. Greta would even exchange phone numbers with the guys with her burner, then send a few trashy messages down the line. What guy is going to tell the police about the hot girl they met that night at the stand after someone boosted a top-of-the-line Range Rover? Blake sometimes swapped out dummy keys at the valet stand, but didn't always have time. They played the valet scam very judiciously from Coconut Grove to West Palm Beach.

Most vehicle theft in America was about stealing boring cars that looked like cheap rentals. The most popular models were what it was all about because the sum of the parts was worth more than any piece-of-shit economy car. It was tough to sell a stolen car, but the parts flew off the chop shop shelves and none of them could be traced. There was no market for expensive car parts because rich assholes didn't care about the price of replacement parts for their rides that cost as much their mechanic's house.

You didn't make much stealing the popular models, and they were almost as hard to boost as the luxury cars. The group Blake was working for—or with—didn't have a name, at least not that he knew of, but he often called it "Nothing but the Best" because that was the only thing on their list. Mostly he just called it "the group." They did everything professionally, or so Blake thought, and this made him think this took a lot of risk out of the game. He always had a prearranged drop-off point near the withdrawal. That was the most important thing.

The Miami area was the perfect place to find hyper-expensive items. All you had to do was cruise a few minutes on I-95 to see dozens of high-end vehicles, not because there were so many rich people in Miami, but because there were so many idiots who wanted to look rich.

What the group did with these top-of-the-line items was above Blake's pay grade. He had no idea what happened to them after he left the vehicle in the designated spot, and he was too smart to ask questions. Through grapevine bullshit, he could only assume that they were being shipped out of the country, probably to Mexico or Colombia. In his estimation, knowledge wasn't power, knowledge was dangerous.

He didn't want to know. He didn't want to know anything about the group except what they wanted him to withdraw, where to drop the item, and where to get paid. He wasn't sure that they were responsible for the kid getting murdered in county lock-up, but they seemed like a creepy bunch, at least what little he knew of them.

He'd only met one person, one time during his eight months working with the group. They got Blake's name from someone he knew. A guy walked up to him while Blake was shooting hoops in a park by his house. After that initial recruitment, they had only communicated via email, and by phones the group provided on a regular and revolving basis.

There'd only been one bump in the road with the group when they tried to pressure him to make more withdrawals due to his initial success rate. Even for the most sinister organization, it was difficult to be overly threatening with a phone call or an email. After meeting with the one representative and a lot of phone conversations, Blake had the feeling that he was smarter than they were. He told the guy on the phone that he was still in high school, that he lived at home, that he had rules to live by dictated by his parents—he didn't mention his father was out of the picture. He sold them his line of goods and they backed off.

Blake lived with his mother, but he'd been paying the rent since he was fourteen. He bought his mom a used car. He demanded she invest eighty percent of her earnings from work, and he made her prove it. She tried to fight him, kicking and screaming, into financial responsibility, but he held the trump card: Blake paid the bills. He could easily afford it.

No one needed to tell him to be discreet about the fortune he was making in his new career. He and his mother had been living in the same modest house since his parents split up five years ago. He didn't have his driver's license and couldn't drive legally. He was scheduled to take the exam in two months but had no interest in buying a vehicle. He rode a bike to school. His bike was his one indulgence. It was a custom-built gravel bike that he'd set up for city riding. He also painted over the custom paint job with olive house paint to greatly lower its theft risk.

He also splurged on computer hardware and software. Blake met with a private tutor once a week to learn programing and other aspects of information technology. He was a smart kid, but he knew his limits, something almost unheard of in kids his age. He was smart enough to understand that he shouldn't try to outsmart criminals capable of murdering a 16-year-old kid because he'd made a simple mistake.

Blake was wise enough to know that he needed an exit strategy, he needed to put a number on just how much he needed to retire from the withdrawal business. He wasn't the type to gamble, a stupid vice he couldn't understand. Many, too many of his friends at school were addicted to online gambling, poker mostly, but for a lot of the little degenerates, it didn't matter, and played every game in town, thinking they were one step ahead of the sports book, the blackjack games, and even the state-sponsored lottery.

He joked to his friends that they should just save time and flush their cash down the toilet, not that any of them had much to flush. He never discussed his business with any of them. Any of them except Greta. They'd sit together occasionally in the school cafeteria during lunch to discuss business, something that raised Blake's stature immensely in the halls and open areas of the school that had more than its share of tough kids.

Fort Lauderdale High School was a perfect example of the American version of the haves and the have nots. Many of the area's wealthiest parents insisted on their children getting a public education, even if it meant they walked through the halls with violent delinquents destined for lives of crime, if they lived long enough to qualify as lives. The rich were quickly abandoning the sinking ship of assaults and dismal academic performance of the once innovative experiment in the American promise of an education for all.

Blake moved between both of these worlds, having grown up poor and a native of the western, rougher part of the city. He'd made it through junior high at one of the worst schools in the district. It could even be said that he had thrived. He graduated with an excellent grade point average, near the top of his class—something not even announced in that place of extremely low expectations. He was particularly adept at avoiding conflict while also not taking shit from anyone.

This was a lesson he'd learned very early in his school career, even before junior high. He learned that you could never back down, even if it meant taking a few punches. Because at those early levels, all it meant was taking a few punches. You fought back, no matter what. Maybe you'd get a black eye or a few bruises. Show fear, and even the most cowardly dog would attack and tear into you.

Always fight back. The predators will move on to easier prey.

And then he met a monster by the name of Wendel Taylor, a six-foot-four-inch menace who loomed over almost every other student at FLHC. They met in the obligatory gym class which was an institution in America education that seemed to be a complete failure, another broken promise.

Why did Blake need to take gym class when he was about as physically fit as a kid could be as his age? He was an avid cyclist and practiced yoga. Among other feats of strength that he could prove, he could knock out twenty clean pull-ups. He definitely didn't need someone to tell him to take care of himself physically, but it was mandated somewhere, by someone, for some reason.

Blake imagined that gym class must be about on the order of prison life. Physical education was little more than a clinic for bullying and intimidation in his experience. He had no reason to believe that this required subject was any different in any other American school. The institution of bullying was an American standard.

"If anyone is trying to figure out why this country is such an incredibly violent place, gym would be a good place to begin looking for answers," Blake was fond of telling anyone who was listening.

Social Darwinism, gladiator school, and fight club were common names for gym and for the most part, all of the insulting things said about gym teachers were true. A less involved adult would be impossible to find than these people who were generally unfit to teach any other subject. Blake knew that gym teachers were the last people he could count for anything resembling protection from the predators.

It was generally a simple matter of not being the lowest member of the gym class food chain, the weakest animal on the Serengeti, the lowest hanging fruit, but sometimes this wasn't enough. Blake always stood up for himself. No one had ever separated him from his lunch money, mostly because he never had money, at least not before he started in the car business. He never considered himself a fighter, but he wasn't afraid of fighting, something an abusive father had literally beat into him.

The trick, once again, was to fight back, always, prove that you weren't at the bottom. This had kept Blake out of trouble through his years at a rough middle school, at least for the most part. High school seemed like it was going to be a little less violent. It was at first, until he had a face-to-face with Wendel Taylor. This kid was a whole new species of bully who possessed a fury that Blake had never seen, even during his father's drunkest fits.

In only the third month at his new high school, Blake had his peaceful coexistence with the school tough guys come to an abrupt end. He and Wendel Taylor were both sophomores, but the other kid must have been older. He was already an adult in appearance, if not in intellect. His intersection with Wendel came in gym class, of course. Blake was on the college preparation program, Wendel just hanging out until he'd be ultimately expelled and sent on his way in life, on to prison, or the victim of gang violence.

Blake knew on the first day that he saw him in gym that he needed to do everything he could to avoid Wendel Taylor. You just tried to be invisible around him, stay in his blind spot, keep off his radar, because there was no getting on his good side, you couldn't be his friend, and you definitely couldn't stand up to him.

It was the typical high school bully routine with the bigger kid trying to humiliate the smaller one, who in this case was Blake. There were on opposing basketball teams when Blake had the stupid idea of playing defense against him. Blake took the ball away from the giant and went all the way down for a lay-up. His moment of glory was going to cost him dearly.

On his next possession, Blake was flattened by a forearm as he drove into the lane. It felt like running head-first into a steel beam. Blake wasn't foolish enough to call a foul, adhering to the age-old gym class adage of "no blood, no foul" even though Wendel had actually drawn blood. He busted Blake's lip just a bit, nothing to worry about. Blake was done playing defense, at least against this sociopath.

Wendel scored a few uncontested points and the tension between the two seemed to have evaporated. Blake didn't get the message that he wasn't supposed to play offense either, because after he hit a three pointer, Wendel came at him head-on.

The bully hit Blake in the face. It wasn't much of a punch. Blake fired back, hitting the man-child in the stomach. And then it was on. Luckily, the fight was stopped before the monster did any serious damage, but Blake knew this wouldn't be the end of it. At least he made it out of the showers after class in one piece.

It wasn't over by a long shot. It wasn't even over for that day.

Until then, all Blake knew about him was that his name was Wendel Taylor. He'd been held back from the year before and was repeating his sophomore year. Blake asked around quite a bit about his nemesis. He heard that Wendel had been held back three times. He was already eighteen years old on his first day this school year. Shit, I'd be angry, too, Blake thought. Wendel lived with his grandmother along with five of his siblings, all younger. The parents were in the wind, evidently. He'd been a good football player in junior high, but had already been kicked off the high school team for fighting. The kid was bad news, very bad news.

Bad News was waiting for Blake when he walked out of school the afternoon of the brawl in P.E. Evidently, Wendel Taylor heard that Blake was making money, a lot of it. Before Blake got to the bike rack outside the west side of the building, Wendel grabbed him from behind. Wendel had two friends at his side who weren't quite at Wendel's level of physical growth, but they both had a few inches and at least twenty pounds on Blake.

"Yo, gimme all you money, bitch."

Blake thought this probably wasn't the right time to correct the grammar of the multi-grade flunk-out artist, but he did anyway.

"'Give me all of your money' is what you should've said," Blake articulating slowly and carefully, as if talking to a child.

It was a stupid and pointless insult. There wasn't even anyone around to witness his clever riposte. Wendel and his goons certainly weren't capable of appreciating it. Blake was terrified, but he hated taking shit off of anyone, another lesson handed down to him from years of suffering abuse courtesy of his worthless and recently absent father.

"I don't have any money, and if I did, why would I give it to you?"

It was true that Blake didn't have any money, nothing more than a few coins in his front pocket. He didn't take money to school because the place was crawling with thieves. But this wasn't thievery, this was robbery.

The two thugs with Wendel stood behind him on either side. He recognized them, but he didn't know their names. One was a senior. He wasn't sure about the other.

Wendel pulled Blake's backpack off his shoulder. When he tried to resist, the other two boys grabbed him roughly by each arm. Wendel emptied out the pack on the sidewalk. There were only books and other school supplies in the bag, nothing that would interest the three half-wit bullies. Blake didn't even have that essential identifying item of youth, a cell phone. His work phone was only for work and he left that at home when he wasn't on a job.

Even the pack wasn't worth stealing. Wendel threw it aside. The other two let Blake loose, but before he could retrieve his bag, Wendel hit him ferociously in the stomach.

"You come to school tomorrow with money, mothafucka, or I gonna break you up."

And with that unlettered threat, the three walked away.

Blake decided that he needed to make a phone call.

It was early November. Blake felt the group owed him a favor after he'd already made dozens of withdrawals. He called his contact and explained his dilemma, not mentioning anything to the guy on the other end of the conversation that if they were going to do something on his behalf, they should show a little restraint, that it wasn't exactly a life-threatening situation for him. Blake had dealt with bullies before, but Wendel Taylor was a new breed of that species, at least in his experience.

They took the pertinent information and told him they'd see what they could do. Then they asked if there was anything else he needed. Anything else? That's when he knew he was part of something big. He was only fifteen years old.

The panel van followed Wendel down the street as he walked home from school the day after Blake had made the phone call. It came to a stop at the curb in front of Wendel. Two men in worker jumpsuits got out from the cargo door. When Wendel ambled by them, one of the men split Wendel's head with a length of pipe while the other muscled the semi-conscious bully into the back of the van. The man with the pipe closed the cargo door behind them and the van drove off.

Wendel wasn't at school the next day or the day after that. Blake never saw or heard about Wendel Taylor ever again. He'd simply disappeared, and absolutely no one seemed to care in the least. There were no "Where's Wendel?" questions among students who all seemed to have the attitude of "good riddance," or other members of his gang who were looking over their own shoulders since the news spread that their leader had vanished into thin air.

Blake was in a mild state of shock. It's not like he missed having a brain-dead monster terrorizing him in gym class for no reason, but he only wanted someone to talk to him, to send a message. It seemed that a message had most definitely been sent. Blake tried to put the affair out of his mind, to think about school and his next withdrawal.

This was precisely what the group had in mind when Wendel Taylor was forced into a sedan at gunpoint so soon after Blake had made his phone call. Wendel's education wouldn't go beyond the third month of his sophomore year, and he'd never bother anyone ever again.

Blake never learned what happened to Wendel Taylor, nor did anyone. The feeling Blake had was one of remorse as well as another stronger feeling of power. He was completely invulnerable. Wendel Taylor was the biggest, strongest, most feared kid in the school. People had witnessed that he'd tormented Blake, and now he was gone. Obviously, this lesson wasn't lost on the other two kids who passed it on to others. Blake walked by one of Wendel's fellow bullies in the hallway four days later and the kid didn't even make eye contact, like he knew something. Now Blake was feared.

Blake was worried that the law would come looking for him as a suspect in Wendel's disappearance. What Blake never understood was that no one gave a shit about the Wendel Taylors of the world. Not even the kid's grandmother cared enough to notify the police when she realized she hadn't seen him in a while. He was an adult, after all, and could fend for himself out there in the jungle, or fall prey to bigger, more powerful animals.

There was the kid who was stabbed to death in county lock-up and Wendel Taylor who may, or may not be dead—although Blake doubted that someone had put Wendel on a bus out of town. In his time with the group, Blake had heard rumors of two more people who may have been murdered because of run-ins with his employer, but it was all just hearsay, urban legends.

***

The drop off areas for items were sometimes in parking garages at shopping malls where the parking was free and there were no attendants. Most of these had video surveillance, but this wasn't a concern. A hat and a pair of sunglasses would thwart identification, and the items weren't in the garages long enough to attract attention. Besides, cameras were everywhere. The garages were used to interrupt helicopter surveillance if the police were somehow tracking the vehicle, a common occurrence in the Miami area. From the time the item hit the drop off area until it was driven away by another member of the team was usually less than five minutes.

Unless the item was truly exotic, the police would never be able to pick it up again when it was driven out of the garage through another exit. For the really high-profile items, they used another protocol.

Blake had just made a withdrawal after he followed a woman into a Pembroke Pines shopping mall who happened to be driving just what he was looking for. He watched her put her keys in the pocket of the loose jacket she was wearing. He skipped ahead of her just as she reached the entrance. He was wearing a Marlins baseball cap, cheap sunglasses, and a track suit, which was about as anonymous as you could get in South Florida. Try giving that description to the police about a suspect and you'd have to wait five minutes before they stopped laughing.

He gallantly opened the door for the woman and fished out her keys as she breezed past, flattered—and distracted—by the attention.

The drop off was in a garage just off I-95 in Hollywood. Blake pulled down into the garage. It was a small garage, much smaller than usual and it was almost empty, which made Blake nervous for a lot of reasons. He parked the item and walked with his head down towards the stairs. Before he got there, a group of five people opened the door coming into the garage from upstairs. They stopped in front of the door talking among themselves. Blake decided to take the elevator so as to limit his exposure with potential witnesses.

He stood waiting with his back to the group in front of the doors to the stairs. They must have forgotten someone or something, because they all went back inside the stairwell area and closed the door behind them. Blake was still waiting for the elevator, considering taking the stairs, when a Dade County sheriff's car pulled down into the garage. From where he stood, Blake couldn't see the item he'd just dropped off, but he heard a car door opening from that direction.

There was only one lawman in the cruiser. There was no way he'd followed Blake; he was sure of it. He pulled into a spot that Blake couldn't see but must have been next to the item. Blake stepped just a bit to his left and looked around the corner of the elevator shaft.

He saw a young woman sit up in the seat next to the cop.

He must have been getting a blow job, was the only thing Blake could think of. That's why he drove into the garage. He was parked directly in from of the item when he shut off the cruiser. From around the passenger side of the item, Blake could see someone stand up pointing a shotgun at the driver's side of the sheriff's cruiser.

Two deafening blasts rang out. Blake saw the girl slump down on the dead cop. The guy with the shotgun opened up the passenger door of the item, and the two drove off. Blake didn't wait around to see what he thought he'd just witnessed. He sprinted for the stairwell. He ran up two flights of stairs and burst through a door into a strip mall. It wasn't crowded enough where he felt comfortable, but there were people. He made his way to the nearest street exit. When he was a safe distance away, he went from a calm walk to a heated sprint.

When he finally stopped running almost two miles from the garage, he walked into a fast-food joint, bought a coffee, and took a seat. He had a message on his phone.

"Burned," was all it said.

One word but he knew the protocol. He left the fast-food joint after he had completely recovered from his sprint. He disposed of the phone as he'd been trained. He went into a tourist shop and bought a new cap and another pair of sunglasses, different from what he was wearing. He walked down into another parking garage and took off the track suit. Underneath he was wearing shorts and a button-down shirt putting the track suit and old glasses and cap into the shopping bag. He'd morphed from clothes that he'd actually wear, to touristy crap he wouldn't be caught dead wearing, an eventuality he hoped wasn't in his near future. He put the old clothing articles in separate trash bins several blocks apart. He set them on top of the bins as he was sure that someone would pick them up within minutes, which was better than the very faint possibility that they'd be discovered by police investigators.

Now all Blake had to do was to make it home to Fort Lauderdale, much easier said, especially when protocol prohibited taking a taxi. He'd never taken a bus in his entire life, but he asked an old woman at a stop how to get where he wanted to go. He had to walk another half a mile and ask several more times before he stepped on a bus going north. He sat in the middle of the bus and tried not to act like he was fleeing from a double homicide.

On that very long bus ride that would take him within a mile of his house, he had a lot of time to panic. He didn't know what he feared most: the police investigation or that perhaps the group thought that he'd led the sheriff to the drop.

Or maybe they considered him just another loose end in a capital crime.

The stories of the murderous nature of the group had suddenly gone from rumor to confirmation for the young car thief. According to protocol, Blake would have no communication from the group for at least one week. He was to follow his normal routine, except for the part of making withdrawals for his employer. He was officially laid off. What Blake really wanted to do was to get the fuck out of Dodge, and by "Dodge" he was thinking about North America. Instead, he went home and sweated.

Even in a place as violent as South Florida, killing a cop is big, big news. No matter what other crimes the police are trying to solve at that moment, cop killers immediately take front and center. It was all over the TV even before Blake went to bed that night, not that he was able to sleep,

Before he left for school the next morning, the news was reporting that a sixteen-year-old girl had been injured in the shooting. There was no mention of her role in the scenario, or even that she had been sitting beside the slain Dade County sheriff. She was in stable condition, whatever the fuck that meant.

He sleep-walked through his morning classes, barely able to understand, it was like his teachers were speaking another language. In the cafeteria at lunch, he sat by himself sipping orange juice and unable to eat a bite.

"Hola, amigo," Greta said as she sat across from him with a tray of food that looked like it was intended for a couple of sumo wrestlers.

Even the presence of the beautiful Greta couldn't do much to pull Blake out of his panic.

"The strong silent type today? I like it," she said, mocking his reticence.

She took two enormous bites out of a burrito before continuing.

"When are we going out again, lover?" she asked, using their feeble code for doing a job together.

Blake really, truly didn't feel like talking, but he thought being a scared little boy would draw more attention.

"Soon."

"Soon? When the fuck is that? Right now is soon for me. Tonight is soon. Tomorrow is soon but not soon enough."

"Soon. I'm working on some shit. You need money or something?" Blake asked.

"Fuck you! Money? It's not that I have anything against it, but you know me better than that," Greta said.

He did.

"Soon, that's all I can say."

"What's up? Something wrong?" Great almost demanded.

'No, I just have some shit to work out."

"Let me help, Blake. Tell me."

He swore that there was just no possible way he was going to implicate her in this mess. He desperately wanted to talk to someone about it, and Greta was at the top of that list, but. But he couldn't. That was also part of the protocol he'd learned from the group, five very simple words anyone could understand: keep your fucking mouth shut. Always.

The police investigation into the murder of the rookie sheriff deputy was a complete mess. Suspects in the murder included the father of the wounded minor, as well had her teen lover, both out for revenge. As it turned out, there was no video of the crime as the seedy shopping mall had neglected their security for months, although this news wasn't released to the public.

Blake was still terrified that the group would put him at blame. Perhaps they'd think he'd been followed by the sheriff. He went over the withdrawal again and again in his mind. There was no way he was followed. Unfortunately, his confidence didn't count for much.

Exactly six days after the shooting, Blake was coming home from school on his bike. A few blocks from his home, a black SUV pulled up alongside him. The mirrored passenger window rolled down and the driver motioned for Blake to stop. He stopped. The driver got out and put his bike in the back. Blake got in the passenger seat. The driver gave him a pair of glasses to put on. The glasses were painted over. Blake could only look down to see his watch.

A half an hour later, the SUV came to a gradual halt after he sensed they'd pulled inside. Someone opened his door and helped him out of the vehicle. Blake saw nothing but the dirty concrete floor. He was planted, almost respectfully, in a chair and left in silence.

Blake was still able to consult his wristwatch, and ten minutes later, he heard footsteps echoing towards him, two or three people.

"Blake, please forgive the present circumstances, but we need to be extremely cautious at this time."

The man spoke English carefully with a Spanish accent. Blake thought that he could've been Cuban, an accent he recognized a bit from a life in South Florida. Colombian? Mexican? He could differentiate Spanish accents to some degree, but doing that through the veil of the subject speaking English was a different matter. He did note the rather sing-song cadence in his speech that he thought was Mexican.

A thick odor of cigar smoke hung over every other scent in what looked to be autobody shop.

The teen knew that the trick with lying was to never change your story. It sounds absurdly simple, but it was the absolute truth. Change your story even a fraction, and you were fucked, especially if you were being interrogated and tortured by professionals.

He was asked to tell them everything that he could remember from that day, starting from the time he got out of bed.

Blake had studied interrogation techniques in the better films and TV police dramas he'd watched. He knew that he needed to stick as closely to the truth as possible, because this was the easiest way to remember what you'd already said under pressure. If they resorted to some form of torture, he knew they weren't really interested in information and simply wanted to inflict suffering. He hoped like hell that it wouldn't come down to that, but if they did, not telling the truth was even easier. They could never verify anything he told them, and they couldn't prove that he was withholding information.

Blake was telling the truth and had nothing to hide, but he still had these thoughts of prevarication running through his mind, trying to determine what his interrogators might not want to hear.

He told them everything that happened that day right up until the county sheriff's deputy pulled into the spot in the garage. That's when he said he ran up the stairs. He told him about the girl in the passenger seat who looked like she was giving the cop a blow job.

"I heard from a kid at school—dad's a cop—that the deputy had his pants around his ankles when he died."

"No shit," was all his interrogator could manage.

Blake never heard that bit about the cop's pants around his ankles, but it might have been true, and it sounded plausible. It was also unverifiable at this time, and even if it weren't true, Blake was just passing along a rumor. Granted, it was a rumor he'd invented.

It also backed up Blake's story that he wasn't followed to the drop. It was just a random coincidence.

"The cop knew the parking garage wasn't very busy," Blake added.

"Maybe."

"It just doesn't seem like the cop was out to do his job with a minor in the seat next to him sucking his cock."

"You saw that?"

"Sure looked like it."

The interrogator paused.

"I wasn't there when it went down, but it seems to me like they could've just driven away with no fuss," Blake said.

"They said it was on. Had to."

"Probably, if they say so."

Blake could tell that they believed him, that his story made sense. He also instantly regretted saying anything prejudicial about the second team.

"There was no security video from the garage, none in the entire shopping center," the interrogator said.

Blake almost blew out a lung full of air in relief. Now they definitely couldn't challenge any part of his story.

"That's a break," Blake said.

"Yeah, for you, too."

"How so?"

How so? What the hell did that mean, Blake thought. Probably just trying to get him to run his mouth until he put his foot in it. He didn't answer.

"If for any reason the police want to talk to you…" he paused.

"Excuse me. I don't mean any disrespect, but can I say something?"

"Sure, kid."

"I may be young, but I'm not a total fucking idiot. I'd never talk to the police. Never. Ever. That's rule number one, right? Never talk to the fucking police. Fifth Amendment. Don't answer any questions. Period. I could give a talk to everyone who works for you precisely why this is all you need to know."

"Maybe you should. Let's hear some of your reasons."

"OK, first of all, talking to the cops can never help. You can't talk your way out of getting arrested and convicted," Blake said. "Lawyers talk, the rest of us do what?"

No takers.

"We shut the fuck up," Blake said, answering his own question.

There was a silence, then Blake heard his interrogator talking to someone else in the room.

"*Quítale las gafas a ese y trae a los dos pendejos. Tengo unas preguntitas para esos imbéciles.*"

He was definitely Mexican, Blake thought. Then someone took off the painted glasses he was wearing. There were two other men in the room, a windowless workshop with a long wooden table along the back wall. There was a door with a window that looked into a warehouse. One of the men was leaving to bring in the two men referred to in the interrogator's last exchange in Spanish.

The interrogator sounded much older, wearier than he appeared, Blake put him at about thirty. Impeccably dressed in a navy suit, white shirt, and no tie, he sat on a folding metal chair and looked to be enjoying the hell out of his Cohiba.

"Excuse me, but in the name of full disclosure, I want to tell you that I speak Spanish," Blake said.

"You want a cookie or something?"

"I just want you to know that I understand what you're saying and that Spanish isn't like some kind of code you can use around me, that's all."

He continued smoking without saying anything but gave an approving nod of the head.

Two men were led in and sat in chairs next to Blake, everyone facing the cigar-smoking interrogator.

"Gentlemen," the cigar smoker said in English, "allow me to introduce everyone. This young one is Blake. These two are Hector and Marcus."

He pointed to the two men sitting next to Blake.

"This is Alonso," he said motioning to the other man. "Alonso heads our security. My name is Sergio. For lack of a better word, let's just say I'm your boss."

Sergio sat back down in his chair.

"Just before you two got here, Blake was explaining how you comport yourself if the police question you. You two know what to say to cops if they ask you questions?"

"I tell them to go get fucked," the one called Hector said in a weak pantomime of defiance and self-confidence he had trouble faking.

"Plead the fifth Commandment," Marcus added with even less conviction.

"Ok. You both need to listen to this. There'll be an exam later," Sergio said, and motioned for Blake to continue.

"So, you can answer a question like 'What is your name?' You really don't have the right not to give that information," Blake said.

When he saw that he had everyone's attention, he continued.

"There's only one more question that you could answer. If he asks, and only if he asks—never volunteer anything—you can tell him what you're doing at the precise spot where you are standing while talking to him. He knows you're there, so it's not like you can deny it. If it's a crime scene and you don't have an answer, just say you were out for a walk."

Blake paused for effect.

"That's it. There is no third question you should answer and there is most-fucking-definitely not a fourth, fifth, or sixth question. You don't answer if he asks you where you were two minutes ago. You talk about right now, right where you're standing. Any other questions and you ask for a lawyer. If he asks how you got there, you ask for a lawyer. If he asks where you are going, you don't say shit except…what?"

"Lawyer," Marcus answered.

"Yes, but not exactly. You don't *ask* for a lawyer, you say you want a lawyer, you fucking demand a lawyer," Blake said. "There's a difference."

"I want a lawyer," Hector repeated.

"That's it. And don't say anything about your Fifth Amendment. Amendment," Blake repeated for the sake of Marcus. "Don't mention the Fifth Amendment because it already sounds like you're guilty. The Sixth Amendment gives you the right to legal counsel, that one's OK to mention."

"You a lawyer? How old is you?" Marcus asked.

"No," Blake said, avoiding the question of his age. "But I read a lawyer's book on the subject, Harvard lawyer. His YouTube video is viral. You need to watch it."

"I'd like to read that book, and watch the video," Sergio said.

The subject quickly changed to the shooting of the cop in the parking garage. Marcus and Hector stuck to the story they gave before, so they obviously weren't complete idiots. Blake thought he had nothing at all to gain by changing his story to challenge theirs by saying that killing the cop was totally unnecessary. The pair made no attempt to sell out the boy, and Blake just wanted all of this behind him and get the hell out of this hellhole, whatever it was.

After almost an hour of questions and answers, Sergio seemed like he had all he needed from the three of them.

"We were incredibly lucky there was no video from the garage, otherwise the cops would be all over this case. They'd have the item, the swap, and they could then backtrack from there. I don't even want to think about that. We need the two of you to lay low for a month. We got separate apartments for Hector and Marcus on the Gulf coast. Alonso's got the details."

Alonso took front and center.

"If you need to let anyone know you're leaving, do it now. Tell them you're going to New York for a few days. Leave your phones here. Once you leave, you don't talk to anyone. Got it?"

Hector and Marcus nodded.

"We go nice places for both of you, comfortable. It's paid for and we'll give you expenses. What we need from you is to lay low, that means minimal contact with the outside world. Just stay in the apartments. Watch TV, jerk off, I don't give a fuck, but stay home. Someone will come by every week to bring you food and anything you need. It sounds bleak but it's for your own good."

Alonso looked directly at the two.

"I need to know right now if you can do this for us, because if you can't, we need to make other arrangements. Can you do this?"

"Yes," Hector muttered.

"Yes, sir," Marcus said.

"Great. Enjoy your time off."

Alonso motioned for the Hector and Marcus to follow him out the door. Sergio held out his hand to Blake to remain seated. When the other three had left, Sergio sat down and pulled leisurely from his cigar like he was sizing up the boy.

"Alonso tells me you've been with us for a while."

"Yes, sir."

"Call me Sergio. He also says you're good. Never a problem and you've made more than your quota consistently. He also told me you resisted requests to step up withdrawals."

Blake remained silent since there was no question.

Blake's reticence wasn't lost on Sergio.

"See, I like that."

Blake sat in silence.

"I like that you didn't apologize or make excuses. He already told me the reasons you gave for not doing more. You were being cautious. Believe it or not, we respect caution, at least I do. Unfortunately, this isn't a universal virtue around here."

Sergio went back to paying full attention to his Cohiba. Blake sat in silence trying to breathe deeply to calm his nerves while wondering what this was about.

Sergio asked Blake a string of innocent questions in Spanish that the boy answered with an imperfect but completely functional fluency. When Sergio's language exam was completed, his returned to English, a language he spoke much better than Blake's Spanish.

"It's hard to believe how few gringos here speak any Spanish. *Jesús*, even the McDonald's signs are in Spanish. Just by the process of osmosis you'd think they'd learn a little," Sergio said.

"I think it's equal parts stupid and racism," Blake said.

"Exactly," Sergio said with a laugh.

He took another pull from his cigar.

"You must be doing OK for a kid your age. Still in school?"

"Sophomore at Fort Lauderdale High."

"Good school?"

"A mixed bag, part gladiator academy and then there's the over-achievers."

"I'm guessing you're in the later half."

Blake didn't answer. It wasn't a question.

"So, what? You're sixteen, making fucking bank. I'm sure you're making more than any of your teachers. If you don't mind my asking, what does a guy your age do with that kind of loot?"

"I take care of my mother. Pay her rent and bills. Mostly I save it."

"What kind of car do you drive?"

"I don't have my license yet. Couple months I take the exam."

Sergio broke out into a hearty laugh, almost choking on his cigar smoke.

"Now that is highly, highly ironic, considering what we pay you to do. Nothing new around here, though. 'As long as they can reach the pedals' is our policy."

Blake kept silent. Sergio stared a hole in his head.

"Alonso told me about you. Said you were smart and you got balls. Now I've seen for myself."

Sergio took a long pull on his smoke.

"Said you had a problem with some asshole at school. Everything good now?"

"Never saw the kid again."

"Really? Lucky you, huh?"

"I don't think it was luck."

"Maybe not, but you let us know if you need anything else. We take care of our people."

Blake was quite aware of that already, for better or worse.

"I just want to say to you that this cop thing, don't think about it. Shouldn't't've happened, but nothing we can do about it now.

Those two do what they're told and stay out of the picture for a while, this will just disappear."

At this point, Blake was too terrified to speak even if he had to.

"This ain't how we like to do things, just so you know. They fucked up, but we got lucky in the end so..."

Sergio motioned for Blake to stand then shook his hand.

"You take it easy for a month, maybe two, then we'll talk again."

With that, he walked away.

Alonso drove Blake home, again with the blacked-out shades. As Blake was getting out, Alonso handed him an envelope and then drove away.

Cash, a lot, at least as much as Blake made in any two-month period. Blake recognized a good-will gesture when he saw one, and especially when it was handed to him in an envelope. Someone was satisfied with his performance. Even the most diabolical, duplicitous organization wouldn't hand out bonuses if they had designs to harm someone, Blake thought.

He wondered about Hector and Marcus, the cop killers, and whether or not their pleasant-sounding exile to the Gulf coast was simply a ploy by the group. Did they have plans to kill them both? The promise of a vacation was the equivalent of parents telling a child that the family dog was sent to live on an idyllic farm in the country. Blake only hoped that his abbreviated testimony that day hadn't in any way contributed to their fate.

Blake literally had more money than he knew what to do with. He had a bank account and a credit card, but he couldn't put much of his earnings in the bank, and he couldn't spend much of it, at least not on anything sensible, something that would appreciate in value. He could blow it all on drugs and living like there was no tomorrow, the usual route for young criminals.

For Blake, money wasn't really the point. He just hated being poor and all of the bad pathologies contributing to it. Teenage pregnancy, lack of education, lack of pride, and a boundless lack of curiosity about the world. His own father was a drunken, ignorant slob. His mother wasn't much better. At least she had only one child whom she couldn't support instead of a brood like so many women of her ilk. The last thing the world needed was more Wendel Taylors.

He discovered that his ex-nemesis had already fathered two children. Wendel Taylor, the eighteen-year-old high school sophomore was a father of two. A man-child without parents begets children without a father, and on and on and on. If Wendel had been killed, at least he wouldn't father any more children.

Rich or poor, Blake was already convinced that he'd never contribute his own DNA to the gene pool. His line would end with him. He never understood why more poor people didn't understand that their best chance at a better life was to remain childless. His own disastrous homelife was more than enough to convince him that he wanted nothing to do with the institution known as the family, at least not in the traditional sense. The group had already done more for him in a few months than his own worthless parents had ever managed.

What the police and social workers could never seem to understand about criminality among the poor was that it often was the result of a lack of police protection. Criminals often became criminals because there was no rule of law in their world to protect them, so they were forced to form groups to safeguard themselves.

200

Prison gangs existed because they offered protection to inmates that the authorities couldn't or wouldn't provide.

A thug like Wendel Taylor acted with complete impunity within the weak authoritative structure of high school. Bullies existed because they were rarely made to pay for their sins, either because of a complete lack of authority, or their victims' fear of reporting them. The reluctance of victims to report bullying was that they feared nothing would be done about it. Report a bully to the school authorities and when they did nothing, the victims would have hell to pay—a violent Catch 22.

When he found himself threatened, Blake made one very short phone call to the group and Wendel Taylor disappeared from his life, perhaps from the face of the earth. He was never intimidated again at Fort Lauderdale High School. What had the cops ever done for him, or school authorities, or his worthless parents?

This left another, thornier question: who could Blake call if he had a problem with the group? Who could Hector and Marcus call? What about the kid murdered in lockup in county? Could they call police? The high school principal? Some other criminal organization?

Laying low was no problem as Blake wanted nothing to do with the group. He considered his opportunities and was leaning towards letting them know that he couldn't do it anymore, that he was too busy with school, or that his mother was ill and needed him. Or the truth, that he was terrified, wanted to break all contact, and never see any of them again.

Only six weeks later he received an email disguised as spam that was the signal for Blake to pick up a new phone to communicate with his contact in the group. Blake was too valuable an asset for the group to keep idle for very long. There were no instructions when

Blake picked up his new phone. He knew the procedure, which was the same as before. They'd send him a description of what they wanted, and he'd find it. When he had the item, he sent a text with one of the prearranged drop-off points which were scattered around the area. He normally chose the nearest drop-off, and someone would be there to take the item, night or day.

It was time for Blake to go back to work. He made his first withdrawal three days after this latest contact. The following day, he received payment and discovered that they'd given him a thirty percent raise. Instead of exalting in his windfall, all Blake could think about was what a paltry sum he received for doing the difficult part of boosting a vehicle that was worth more than the combined annual salaries of many Miami couples.

He wasn't even a legal adult and had already made more this year than his mother had ever made in a single year. It was only March. He thought that he probably shouldn't be complaining about what he was making, especially after this increase in his income that he hadn't requested. If he didn't like it, he should quit.

He liked it. He wasn't addicted to the thrill of stealing, but he loved getting paid for what he did. He loved earning. Making money made him feel useful. Paying his mother's bill every month gave Blake a sense of direction that overcame whatever fear he had of the police for whom he had little respect, at least as far as their ability trip him up. What he never suspected was that someone from the group would give him up to the authorities.

From one of the gyms he patrolled regularly, he found a lead on a luxury sedan on his list. He already had a dummy key and was waiting for the following Monday morning when he knew the guy would be working out. He didn't have to break into the locker as his contact had a master key for him to use after Blake explained his process a bit and assured him that it wouldn't blow back on him. He swapped out the keys and drove the item to the drop. The unlucky car owner would never link the gym to the auto theft as he thought he still had his key.

Blake pulled into the strip mall surface lot and found the aisle where he was told to park the item. The lot was less than half full with few pedestrians in sight. As Blake approached the spot, a black Crown Victoria pulled out of a space directly in front of him. He slammed on his brakes. Blake looked in his rear view and saw another sedan coming up quickly behind him. Without taking the car out of drive, Blake opened his door and jumped out. His car rolled into the Crown Victoria, crashing into the side and trapping the driver inside. From the passenger side he could see someone already out of the car and looking over the top in his direction. Their eyes met, but Blake didn't look long.

He ran between the parked cars, his heart beating wildly from fear and adrenaline. The alarm from his vehicle was screaming loudly, adding to the chaos. He could hear another vehicle speeding around the lot in his direction, and then a police unit with siren blaring and lights flashing pulled into the entrance to the lot.

There were four police vehicles in this operation, but they had no one on foot, obviously anticipating that any chase would be in in their vehicles. Blake had seen enough vehicle pursuits on television to know that those always went badly for the criminals. He was already dressed for a run in his athletic shoes and tracksuit. He ran to the last row of parking and jumped over a short hedge.

He landed in the street with oncoming traffic moving towards him. He ran against the traffic on the shoulder. He saw that one of the unmarked cruisers was attempting to turn left out of the parking lot to move in his direction against traffic. Traffic was heavy. and even with the siren blaring and lights flashing, the cop car couldn't move far as Blake jumped another hedge and was in the parking lot of the adjacent strip mall. He ran towards the stores. This lot was separated by another hedge from the lot where he'd ditched the car. He saw the other police vehicles leaving the first lot. Blake hurdled this hedge and ran to the back of the strip mall where he left the item. There was a narrow alley along the back side of the mall for deliveries and garbage disposal.

A chain-link fence separated this mall from yet another mall behind it. Blake scaled the ten-foot fence and was in another back alleyway. He found an open door to a supermarket and ran through the storage area. An employee saw him enter but didn't seem to care that Blake wasn't allowed there. After only a few steps Blake was at the door leading into the supermarket. He stopped, removed his jacket, sweatpants, and ball cap. He walked through the swinging doors and into the crowded supermarket wearing khaki shorts and a button-down long sleeve shirt. He also had a small backpack and had stuffed the track suit and cap inside. He grabbed a few bananas and apples. He paid for them at the cash register and walked outside.

There was no sign of police in the parking lot, which was a relief, but Blake had nowhere to go. Welcome to suburban Miami where it's impossible to walk anywhere. Just trying to walk in this car-centric area would attract a lot of attention. He considered taking a bus, but they were few and very far between. A taxi was out of the question. He thought of calling someone, but he'd already ditched his phone in the alley and had thrown the card in another dumpster. Pay phones were a thing of the past, as uncommon as walking.

There was a cinema in the strip mall where Blake thought he might be able to find a pay phone. As he approached, he saw people in line buying tickets. He stepped behind them and got a ticket for the next feature. It was some children's cartoon thing, but he hadn't been to the movies in forever. He found a pay phone, made a quick call, bought a ticket, and after loading up on popcorn and a lemonade, he took a seat in the cool, dark theater.

All he could think about during the mindless entertainment was that Lee Harvey Oswald was caught in a movie theater.

Ten minutes before the end of the feature, he walked out into the glaring late-afternoon sunshine and waited on the curb. Greta pulled up two very long minutes later.

"Am I late?" she asked as she made her way out of the strip mall.

"Not at all. I'm just freaking the hell out," Blake said.

Greta pulled out on to the main thoroughfare and headed north.

"That was some sort of miracle. I was dropping off an item in strip mall on the other side of the theater and was ambushed by the cops."

"What?"

"Obviously a set up. They were waiting for me."

"How'd you get away? A chase, like in the movies?"

"I ran. Rolled the car I was in right into the unmarked car blocking me and took off. I don't think any of them ran after me. They stayed in their vehicles."

"Someone definitely hung you out to dry on this. What're you gonna do?"

That was a very tough question that Blake had been considering even as he was running through the strip mall parking lot. The "who" was also on his mind. Only two people were supposed to know about the drop off locations besides Blake.

It operated like this: Blake would send a text with numbers indicating his drop-off location. The number-coded drop off locations were from a list that changed every four days and represented six different zones in the various counties in the area. This location was in the north of Dade County.

The text was forwarded to whoever was picking up the item, and who was never in direct contact with Blake. He'd send a confirmation code when he was on the way with the item. The first message was supposed to be at least thirty minutes before the withdrawal took place. There were other contingencies, but these usually required that Blake had to spend more time and cover more distance in the item, raising his level of risk. Sometimes opportunities presented themselves and he had to act.

Either the dispatcher had given him up to the police, or the other one or two drivers assigned to pick up the item.

If it was the dispatcher, this meant that the group was out to put him in jail, which seemed highly unlikely. If they had a problem with him, they wouldn't involve the police. The more probable explanation was that the drop-off driver had been picked up by the police before he picked up the vehicle and gave up the location. Blake thought this was unlikely, but the most plausible scenario he could think of.

Fucking amateurs! What part of "never talk to the police" didn't they understand? Blake thought.

"Pack overnight bags for both of us. We're spending two days at a luxury spa in Miami," Blake told his mother on Greta's phone as she drove to Fort Lauderdale.

His mother argued with him. She had things to do. She didn't have time to go away right now. Why hadn't he given her a heads up? What was going on?

"I'll be home in twenty minutes. Be ready. For once in your life can you just shut the fuck up and do what I ask?" Blake yelled before hanging up.

He didn't trust his mother with the truth, and he knew she'd panic if she thought she might be in any danger.

Blake still had Greta's phone in his hand when it rang.

"Your mother?" Greta asked.

Blake answered without checking the caller.

"Who is this?" Blake asked.

"Do you recognize my voice?"

"Yes," Blake answered.

It was Alonso.

"Where are you?" Alonso asked.

A moment of silence.

"OK, it doesn't matter where you are. Just don't go home. I have people on the way there now."

"Why?"

"You got burned. It was the second team. We had someone else there at the drop who saw the whole thing."

"How the fuck did you get this number?"

"I have all your numbers, it's what I do. I know you work with this woman. Didn't expect you to answer, but here we are."

Blake was trying to think of how Alonso could have broken into his phone.

"Just to be safe, I sent people to your house."

"My mother is there."

"When was the last time you talked to her?" Alonso asked.

"Like two minutes ago."

"Relax, just don't go home until I call you. Got it?"

Blake didn't answer.

"Think this through, Blake. If we wanted you gone, we wouldn't have called the cops. You should know that by now."

Blake knew that by now.

"Almost there now. They're coming to my house?"

"Just give me a couple minutes and my guys will be there."

Blake hung up without answering and called his mother. No answer.

Alonso called back.

"We're there now. Hang back. My guys got this."

The second team pair were friends of Marcus and Hector and suspected Blake for their disappearance and probable execution, their punishment for killing the sheriff's deputy. The group had underestimated the allegiance of this second team to their friends. After setting Blake up and then witnessing the botched arrest, they went to his house, arriving minutes before Alonso's men.

They beat his mother senseless and were waiting for the son to return home.

Alonso's two men came in on the stealth through the patio door, the big guy carrying a pistol and his partner with a sawed-off shotgun. The two intruders were standing over the woman when the armed men surprised them. The big guy cracked one of their skulls but good with the butt of his pistol. He dropped in a heap, cracking his head even harder on the ceramic tile floor. The other intruder dropped to his knees and raised his hands over his head.

"Don't kill me," he pleaded.

"On the floor, face-down, hands behind your back," he was ordered.

The big guy cinched his hands together with a zip tie, then he kicked him in the head.

Greta pulled past Blake's house and he had her park a few houses away. He jumped out of the car, ignoring Alonso's instructions. He sprinted around back to the patio door that opened into the kitchen. It was wide open. He made it through the kitchen but was stopped in the doorway by the big guy who almost filled it.

"Blake?" he asked, "I'm with Alonso."

He grabbed Blake by one shoulder; he had a gun in his other hand.

"Blake, it's bad, but I need you to be cool. Alonso will be here. He'll take care of this."

"Where's my mother? Blake asked, not wanting to know the answer.

It was bad? How bad?

Alonso's man let him pass through.

His mother was lying on the floor in the entryway; the side of her face covered with a towel; the top of her dress stained with blood.

There was a man on the tiled floor in the living room who looked dead, his body sprawled at an impossible angle on the floor, his head lying in a pool of blood, but he was breathing. Another man was lying on the floor face-down with his hands behind his back and cinched with a nylon zip-tie.

Alonso arrived with three men besides the two already in the house.

"We need to get everyone out of this house," Alonso said.

He gave Blake time to gather some essentials. Blake was thinking clearly enough that he remembered leaving Greta on the street. He called and sent her away. They'd meet later, he promised.

"I know it's fucked up Blake, but this is just too much to explain if the neighbors heard anything," Alonso said. "With no one home, they'll forget about it. There's nothing we can do now."

Blake had no idea how they'd explain his mother's death; he hadn't processed any of it yet.

Blake opened the attached garage door and Alonso's man drove his SUV inside where they put the two prisoners. They drove off immediately. Two other members of his team stayed behind to manage the other body, Blake's mother.

Alonso told Blake to ride with him, leaving a discreet interval after the SUV with the prisoners.

Alonso pulled out a pair of painted sunglasses.

"Put these on. You're better off not knowing where this place is, trust me."

Blake trusted Alonso, at least now he did.

When Blake removed the glasses, they were inside a large warehouse with several other vehicles parked to one side. One of the prisoners was tied with wire to a metal chair with the other lying on the floor, Blake couldn't tell if he was dead or alive.

Alonso conducted the interrogation, and it didn't take him long to get everything he needed.

Hector, Marcus, and these two who set Blake up had grown up together, entered into crime together in some shithole neighborhood in the far western reaches of Miami. They somehow managed to make their way into the group.

"The truly mind-bogglingly stupid thing about your action is that your two friends are alive. We sent them to lay low. Now what? Do we need to kill them, too?"

The prisoner didn't respond.

"There's no fucking hope for you at this point. You do realize that, right?" Alonso asked.

The prisoned seemed to understand his fate.

"But your friends don't have to die. They had nothing to do with this. We know that. They haven't talked to anyone."

Alonso stood up.

"Am I right?"

"We didn't talk to them," the prisoner managed to say. "We heard they was dead."

"Who else knows about this?"

"It was just us."

Alonso sat down again.

"Good. You want to send a message to anyone before…before?" Alonso asked, not articulating the fate of the prisoner.

The kid said he wanted to write a letter to his girlfriend, which Alonso allowed him to write. He found a pen and paper and gave him a few minutes to put down his last words.

In the presence of the condemned, Alonso asked Blake if he wanted to end the life of the man who had ratted him to the police and then savagely beat his mother to death, two offenses punishable by death in the code they lived under. Alonso advised him against this.

"Just giving you the option, but you don't need to carry that around with you."

Blake wanted no part in the execution, but he said nothing either way. He couldn't speak.

"Don't worry. Someone will take care of it."

Alonso held the letter in his hand as he stood in front of the condemned man. He read it, then ripped it into small pieces and threw it in the prisoner's face.

"You truly are a fucking idiot. Your gal will be just fine without you. Maybe I'll send Blake over to her house, take her out, show her a good time."

Alonso turned his back on the prisoner and led Blake out of the warehouse. In front of the door, a luxury sedan was idling. A backseat window lowered. Sergio waved Alonso and Blake over.

"Get in, Blake," Sergio said.

The door opened and Blake got in beside his boss.

"This is some monumentally fucked up shit for a kid your age. I should know, my parents were both killed in Mexico when I was young, not as young as you, but too young for my parents to be murdered," Sergio said. "Ugh, not like there's ever a good age for that. It's just something we seem to accept now in Mexico. *La muerte*. Death. It's like our new national lottery."

Blake sat in silence, barely able to understand the conversation.

"This shouldn't have happened and I know there's nothing I can say or do to make it up to you except to say that you are one of us. Anything you need, just ask."

Blake didn't ask.

"As inadequate as these words are, I am truly sorry for your loss, Blake."

Blake broke his silence.

"Thanks."

Through everything he'd been through in the past twenty-four hours, Blake felt like he'd broken the surface of the water after being submerged for too long, able to breathe again. He was part of the group. He was one of them. With his mother dead, his father who the hell knew where, he was now part of a family for the first time in his life.

Family was everything.

CHEKOV'S GUN

"Never place a loaded gun onstage if it isn't going to go off."

   - Anton Chekhov

Between murders, suicides, and accidents there were 45,000 firearm deaths in the USA in 2021.

What would Chekhov say about introducing 400 million guns onstage?

The iron gate to Wally's Pawn Shop opened with a buzz from an electronic sensor. Above the register was the obligatory Confederate flag flanked by posters championing NRA doggerel. The kid approached the display case of semi-automatic rifles.

"Afternoon," Wally said. "Need something?"

"Just looking," the kid whispered.

"Gotta be eighteen."

"Today's my birthday."

"Congratulations," Wally said. "Whaddya after?"

"Something for self-defense."

And mowing down as many bullying classmates as possible, he fantasized.

Wally put an AR-15 on the counter.

"This'll do the trick. Thirty round magazine. Semi-auto."

Wally winked, implying that the "semi" was a mere formality.

Purchasing an assault rifle was legal for the teenager; he'd have to wait another three years to buy a beer.

He'd never been on a date, never kissed a girl…or a boy for that matter, and never would since he'd already set a date for the end. He had no hobbies or interests in anything beyond TV and video games. Hated school, that much he knew. Thought he was smarter than most of his idiot classmates, just wasn't into books. He was street smart, something people who never read often said to justify their quasi-illiterate existence.

If "street smarts" meant anything and if he possessed this virtue, it served little purpose in school. He was a poor student and got picked on, making him dream of invisibility. He was friendless, awkward, painfully shy, and harbored violent thoughts towards everyone at school.

He never raised his hand in class, but his history teacher called on him anyway.

"Who did America fight in the Second World War?"

"Communists?" he answered with another question.

There was faint laughter, but his nemesis, a boy he'd known his entire life and the best student in the school sat silently next to him.

"John?" the teacher asked of his adversary.

"Germany and Italy were the axis powers," his answer confident but almost apologetic.

John's ease filled the kid with a murderous rage. Know-it-all jerk-off. He wanted to ask what "axis" meant but couldn't endure further ridicule. To his relief, someone asked the question without being mocked. Even the teacher struggled with the explanation. He'd look it up at home.

He planned to go to the shooting range after school for one final rehearsal, but after a few clicks on his computer, he was enthralled by the saga of WWII. One battle led to another harrowing chapter and before he knew it, he passed out on his bed after seven solid hours. He'd never studied so much in his life.

He woke up early. This was the day he was going to do it, but instead of implementing his plan, spent another thirty minutes reading about the siege of Stalingrad. Of all things, he was excited about history class.

He sat down next to John, but today he dared to speak to him.

"John, how do you know so much about World War Two?"

"I don't, really," John said without false modesty.

"You know more than any of us, maybe more than Mr. Holder."

"I've read a few books about it," John said.

This revelation hit him like a bullet. He just needed to read to spare himself the constant humiliation of ignorance, of not knowing. School guidance counselors urged him to apply himself but never explained exactly how. He had another question for his classmate.

"Do you like school?"

"Hell no," John said without a moment of hesitation. "I can't wait for the new deal."

"What's that?"

"Nothing here means anything once we leave. The people you think are cool will have to start from scratch. Popular kids and bullies are in for a big shock, like royalty having their lands confiscated. It'll be like a new deal in a card game.

Three weeks until graduation, then a new life. He'd try harder this time, make something of himself.

Chekov's gun doesn't have to be fired. With the receipt, you can get a full refund at Wally's.

ABOUT THE AUTHOR

John Scheck has lived in four countries on three continents. In no particular order, these include eight years in Lower Queen Anne in Seattle; the Miraflores district of Lima, Peru, during a university program; the Glyfada area of greater Athens, Greece, as part of his short and distinguished service in the U.S. Air Force; and now the Ruzafa neighborhood in sunny Valencia, Spain, is home.

His other books include the collection of humor essays *Nothing Personal* along with the novels *La Frontera Saga*, *Twenty-Seven Calls*, and *Criminal Code*.